Bronze Skies

Dangerous Times, Book Three

by

Ilona Fridl

This is a work of fiction. Names, characters, places, and incidents are either the product of the author's imagination or are used fictitiously, and any resemblance to actual persons living or dead, business establishments, events, or locales, is entirely coincidental.

Bronze Skies: Dangerous Times, Book Three

Cover Art by *Rae Monet, Inc. Design*

The Wild Rose Press
PO Box 706
Adams Basin, NY 14410-0706
Visit us at www.thewildrosepress.com

Publishing History
First Vintage Rose Edition, 2011
Print ISBN 1-60154-931-8

Published in the United States of America

"Will you tell me where Vic Houston is?"

Jake nodded toward an old blue Oldsmobile. "He's working under the hood over there."

"Thanks, Jake." The smell of gas, grease, and rubber hit Tom's nose as he made his way to the Olds. He saw Vic with a wrench, tightening something in the engine. Tom leaned against the fender. "Vic, do you have a moment?"

Vic looked surprised, and Tom noticed his grease-grimed hand clench the wrench tighter. "What do you want, Shafer?" His voice was rough.

"I didn't come here to fight you, but before I leave to go back to base, I have something to say. If I hear you've hurt Pam in any way, I will find you."

Vic's fingers bunched the dirty cloth that covered the radiator grill. "I don't plan to hurt Pam, but that doesn't mean I won't try to date her. And the big-time flyboy didn't bring any charges against me. Are you too chicken?" He spit on the floor by Tom's feet.

Dedication

To my family and friends.
To my mentor, Kathie Giorgio.
To my great editor, Nan Swanson.
This book is dedicated with honor and respect
to the men and women
who served in the armed forces, especially
to the brave pilots of the Eleventh Army Air Corps
out of Elmendorf, Alaskan Territory.

Chapter 1

Summer, 1941
Juneau, Alaska

Tom Shafer glanced down to Juneau's airfield. "I see my cousin Hank has fallen asleep on top of the hood of the car. This is too tempting."

Sitting behind Tom, Ernie Collins knew what the young army pilot was going to do. "Damn it, Tom, don't buzz him! I'll get blamed for it."

Maneuvering the small mail airplane into position, Tom grinned over his shoulder at Ernie. "Don't worry. I'll tell them I made you sit in the dummy seat."

The early morning Alaska sun was well up in the sky. Below, Hank was stretched out on the Hudson's hood and windshield, using it as a lounge chair. His white navy uniform ruffled in the summer sea breeze, the cap over his face.

Centering the plane on his target, Tom picked up speed while dropping, pulling up just in time. He circled around and saw Hank was on the ground, his white cap rolling off on the other side of the car.

Laughing, Tom headed for the landing strip and brought the plane coasting toward the mail office, as he had done so many times before he joined the Army Air Corps. The post office agent, Bill Wright, stood next to the door, hands on hips and a less than pleasant look on his face. "Ernie! What the hell do you think you're doing? You know you have government property on that airplane!"

Tom hopped off the wing. "Yeah, and a part of

1

the property is me."

Mr. Wright started, then smiled and held out his hand. "Tom, it's great to see you again. How's everything in Anchorage?"

"Busy, as usual. But for once Hank and I managed to get leave the same week. By the way, don't be hard on Ernie. He was just a passenger, and he didn't know I was going to pull that stunt."

Mr. Wright glanced at Ernie, who wore a contrite demeanor. "I'll let it go this time, only because Tom was one of our best pilots."

Ernie sighed. "Thanks, boss." He started unloading the sacks of mail from the cargo.

Tom paused for a moment in helping him. "Is Pam still working at Millie's?"

"Yes, she is. Are you going to stop over?"

"I plan to."

Hank stalked toward them, knocking the dirt off his cap and uniform. "Still doing those circus tricks, I see. Damn it, Tom, you practically scared the shit out of me!"

They scuffled, then threw their arms around each other, and Tom clapped Hank on the back. "My God, it's good to see you. It's been almost a year, with us not getting leave at the same time."

Saying their goodbyes to Ernie and Mr. Wright, the boys headed to the car. Tom looked around and took a whiff of the new-car smell as Hank started it up. "Wow, this is a great Hudson. Yours?"

Hank snorted. "I couldn't get this on a sailor's wages. I borrowed it from my dad."

"Whew, the theater must be doing better now. They were still behind, a year ago."

"It looks like we're finally coming out of the depression, although even then people still came to the movies."

"How is the restaurant doing? I heard Mrs. Hutton retired and went to Los Angeles to live with her son."

"Jen has taken over the business end, and Aunt Amelia is our cook—and a good one, since she was working with Mrs. Hutton all those years."

Tom shifted on the seat. "I'm going to miss Mrs. Hutton. Anything new?"

"The folks are getting into stage again. Mainly at the insistence of your mother."

Tom chuckled. "Not many can say no to her. I've tried countless times. I guess everyone will be at the theater, since this is the busy season, but first, Hank, can you drop me off at this corner? I want to go to Millie's."

Hank smiled knowingly. "Going to see Pam first, uh-huh. Don't be long. Everyone is going to grill me when I get back without you."

"Stay in the kitchen. I'll be there in fifteen minutes."

Hank waved as he drove off.

Tom whistled happily, walking on air down the street. It had been six months since he'd visited with the golden-haired beauty who had enchanted him so in high school. It was her father who got him into flying. After Mr. Wright found Tom was a natural pilot, Tom got his flying license when he was sixteen and worked as an air mail pilot through the rest of his high school years. Upon graduation, he went right into the Alaska Defense Command and had already made it to the rank of lieutenant. Now he was stationed at Elmendorf Field outside Anchorage.

Tom slid through the door at Millie's. Most of the breakfast crowd had cleared out, and he caught sight of the willowy blonde, her back toward him, and recognized the French roll of her hair under the crisp white uniform cap. He glanced at the gray-haired Millie behind the counter and put his index finger to his lips. Millie smiled and nodded.

Tom tiptoed to the big Wurlitzer jukebox by the

side of the dance floor and fed it a nickel. Strains of "Serenade in Blue" drifted over the dining area. He watched Pam turn, and her eyes lit up with surprise and happiness. She ran to him, and he caught her in an embrace.

"Tommy, you're home!" She put her hands on either side of his face and looked at him like she couldn't quite believe her eyes. "You get my letters?"

He put his fingers over hers. "I've kept every one. Reading them is almost like having you with me. I'm sorry I haven't answered all of them, but we've been working hard at the airfield." He gave her a quick kiss on her forehead, and he could feel his body warm. "Can you come to the house tonight for dinner? I'll check with my folks, but I'm sure it will be all right."

"Oh, yes! My father is picking me up, and I'll go home to change after work. I can walk over there by six."

Suddenly he heard, "Well, look who's here—the flyboy!"

Tom broke from Pam and glared at the intruder. "Vic! What are you doing here?"

A big angry-faced bully, Vic Houston gazed at Pam. "I wanted to talk to *her*."

Pam put her hands on her hips and tapped her foot. "What do you want?"

Grinding his back teeth, Vic growled, "I want you to be my girl. I'd show you a better time than a pansy flyboy, any day." The arm he put around her was pushed away as she winced and pulled back.

Tom wadded Vic's shirt in his fist and leaned toward his face. "You leave her alone!"

Vic's foul breath stung Tom's nose. "Who's going to make me?"

In a second, Millie had pushed them apart. "I don't put up with this in my restaurant. If you don't want me to call the police, you stop now!"

Looking first at Millie, her eyes flashing, then at Pam and Tom, Vic huffed and stomped out the door.

Millie shook her head. "Be careful of him, you two. That's one unhappy person." She went back to the counter.

Tom glanced at Pam. "I didn't know he knew who you were."

Her mouth formed a tight line. "We were both at a party, and I made the mistake of dancing with him."

Tom swore under his breath. "I wish I could stay more than a week. I didn't know you would have a problem like this." He gently held her shoulders. "You need me here."

She sighed. "I can manage. With all the tension between America and Japan, you're going to be needed to help keep the Japanese out. My father's sure we'll get into this war that's raging around the world. My problem isn't that important."

"It is to me." He stirred her hair as he spoke in her ear. "Go to your family or mine if he tries anything." He gave her a quick kiss. "See you tonight. I'd better go before I get you in trouble with Millie."

Her eyes, the blue of a robin's egg, sparkled. "I'll be there."

Waving toward Millie, he left the restaurant. Tom thrust his hands into his pockets and resumed whistling on his way to the theater. It was a feeling more than anything else that made him turn around by one of the alleys, just as Vic was about to nab him. "What do you want, Vic? You run out of school kids to pick on?"

Pushing Tom against the building, Vic glared at him. "Listen, Shafer, if you want to keep healthy, stay away from Pam."

Tom looked heavenward. "I think we should leave that up to Pam. There are plenty of other girls here in Juneau. Some might even want to be with you."

Vic pulled back his fist, and Tom's army training kicked in, blocking the incoming knuckles and giving Vic a low blow to the solar plexus. Vic doubled over, and Tom smashed his knee into Vic's face. Vic flew back and slid into a seated position at the base of a lamppost.

Tom tossed Vic a handkerchief. "Your nose is bleeding. I'd take care of that, if I were you." He continued on his way.

Behind him, he heard Vic. "This isn't the end of this, Shafer."

Ignoring Vic, he rounded the corner to the large white building that housed the Golden North Theater and Restaurant. It looked a little more shabby than when he was a kid. The family had really had to scrape to make ends meet during the early thirties, when the depression hit hardest here in Juneau, but things seemed to be coming back now.

Tom went around to the rear and slid into the kitchen of the restaurant and bar, where his Aunt Amelia Carter was working her magic over the stove and oven. Aromas of fresh bread and hot stew wafted to his nose. Because of her late mother's harsh treatment of her, Amelia had always preferred working in the kitchen, away from the crowds. She'd never gotten over her shyness, but she gave Tom a quick hug. "It's good to have you home for a while." She smiled and looked down quickly.

Hank sat on one of the chairs, munching an apple.

"Where's my dad and mom?" Tom asked Amelia.

"I think they're still rehearsing in the theater."

"See ya later, Auntie A." Tom and Hank made their way across the dining and bar area and through the swinging doors to the lobby, where they could hear angry voices coming from the theater.

"Why can't I play Yukon Lil now? I'm as good an actress as you are, and I'm closer to her age. You're getting gray." The plaintiff was Tom's seventeen-year-old sister, Emily. She was directing her displeasure at her mother, who gripped the back of a prop chair. Tom's dad appeared from backstage.

"Addy, count to ten slowly." He turned on his daughter. "Emily, that was rude and disrespectful. Apologize to your mother now!"

Emily sighed. "I'm sorry, Mother. But I do think I could take on the larger roles now."

Dan Hanson, who had been their director ten years ago, stood. "Addy, I think she's as good an actress as you are. She can take on the older parts."

His mother whirled to glare at Dan. "Now, wait a minute—"

Tom piped up from the back. "I can see things haven't changed much since I left."

Everyone turned and said, "Tom!" at the same time. His mother got to him first, and he resisted the urge to pick her up and swing her around. She was a good seven inches shorter than he was. He hugged her, and she cupped his face in her hands, her deep brown eyes glowing. "I've missed you so."

His father clapped him on the back. "Good to have you home, son."

Emily stood back with a grin. "Well, it looks like my tormentor is back."

"My, how you've grown since I left. Little Em is getting big for her britches." Tom laughed and ducked as she swung a fist at him. "Did I hear right, Dad? You and Uncle Josh have gotten your musical on stage?"

Dan Hanson came up the aisle. "They did. And it's an excellent piece of work. We've been performing it for a couple of months now."

Tom warmly shook his hand. "It's good to see

you again, Mr. Hanson. It's been a long time."

"There wasn't a whole lot of work coming up in Hollywood, so when your folks offered this to me again, I took it."

Tom turned to Hank. "Where are your parents and Jenny? They're usually here."

"They all went over to the mercantile to order a few things. They should be back in a little while."

Tom's dad shook his head. "How did you two manage to both get leave at the same time?"

Hank shot a grin at Tom. "It took some devious finagling on our parts, but we did it."

Emily broke in. "Did Hank tell you that Jen is engaged to Chase now? They plan to get married in June. Do you think you two can come?"

The boys glanced at each other. Hank laughed. "Can we get a word in edgewise? We can see."

Tom turned to his father. "I stopped at Millie's for a moment on the way over and asked Pam if she could have dinner with us. Is that okay?"

His dad gave him an amused grin. "I think you should have asked us first, but we can make room."

Tom punched him on the arm. "Thanks, Dad."

Tom's mother was examining the right knee of his uniform trousers. "Is that blood? Emily, run get some cold water, a towel, and a sponge from the kitchen." Emily went quickly up the aisle.

Looking down, Tom assured her, "Don't worry, Mom, it's not mine." At her evil eye, he continued, "I ran into Vic at Millie's, and he seems to think Pam is his girl." Tom went on to tell them about the confrontation.

Emily came back with a basin, and his mother soaked the stains. She shook her head. "The stain is coming out. Tom, I wish you wouldn't fight in the street."

"I was just defending myself. You know how Vic was in school."

8

His father registered concern. "I would tell Pam to watch herself. Those are the kind who never take no for an answer."

Tom frowned. "She said she was going to walk over to our house after work. Should I walk her over and back?"

"It's still a late daylight, and she lives only a block and a half away. She should be all right. You can walk her home."

"Dad, I told her if she was ever in trouble she should go to her family or ours."

His mother nodded. "Good idea. With that type of man, you can never be too careful. Believe me, I know." She took the towel and dried the excess water off Tom's trousers. "There. I got it out."

Tom still worried about the possibility of Vic hanging around Millie's, but at least Mr. Wright was going to pick his daughter up after work. *It would be a good idea for him to do that every day.* Tom shared his concern with Hank as the two cousins finally left the theater and walked to their homes, next door to each other in a quiet residential section of Juneau. Growing up so close, the boys had always felt more like brothers. They discussed the problem, but without any definite conclusions.

When their dappled, tree-lined street came into view, the two white clapboard houses with the green trim looked the same as they ever did. The stately maple and oak trees in the respective yards brought to Tom's mind the carefree summer days in the branches.

Laughing, Tom punched Hank on the arm. "Remember when we used to play pirates and shoot rubber balls at each other from those trees?"

"The slingshots really got a workout, didn't they? And Dad never did find out that you were the one who broke the side window. That would be some good blackmail to hang over you."

Shaking his head, Tom retorted, "There's enough dirt on you I could bring up. Like the time you flattened my mom's prize rosebush. She never found out who did that."

As they reached home, Hank clapped Tom on the back. "See you tomorrow, cuz!"

Tom smiled and waved as he went up the driveway.

****

Pam sat on the end stool at the counter, waiting for her father. Shaking out a cigarette from its pack, she lit it and pulled the glass ashtray toward her as she tried to sort out her confused feelings. It had been six months since she had seen Tom, and he hadn't answered all her letters. *Maybe he told the truth when he said he was busy.* She truly wanted to believe that, but when the days and weeks went by between letters from him, she began to wonder if he still cared for her. One weekend she'd gotten so lonely she decided to go to the dance with her friends. That's where she encountered Vic.

"Hello, princess, are you ready?" broke into her thoughts.

She brightened. "Hi, Daddy. Yes, I am." Pam stamped out her cigarette, then waved to Millie as she went out the door and to the waiting Buick, where she slid into the passenger's seat. Her father started up the car again and glanced at her as he turned it toward home. "Did Tom stop by today?"

"Yes. He asked me over for dinner at his folks' home tonight. Is that all right?"

"You know it is." He hesitated. "You seem pensive. Is everything going well?"

"It's about Tom. I was very happy to see him today, but I wonder if the time apart has changed things. He doesn't answer all my letters, and sometimes I do get lonely. I keep thinking maybe we should date others."

"You could bring up those concerns to him this week. See where you stand with one another."

Pam stared out the passenger window and wondered whether she should bring up the subject of Vic, then rejected the idea. *It'll be better not to worry Dad about that. Maybe I made it clear to Vic that I wasn't interested in him.*

When they arrived home, she greeted her mother and her brother, Ted, before hurrying upstairs to change out of her uniform. Suddenly there was the old feeling of electric excitement she used to have in high school when she readied for a date with Tom. She unpinned her French roll and brushed out her hair. Then she carefully rolled and pinned the sides and top, letting the remaining hair fall down her back and curl under. After a careful application of lipstick and powder, she slipped her compact into her purse and headed to the stairs.

Her mother met her by the door. "Your father tells me you're going to the Shafers' for dinner. Tell Tom to stop over sometime this week. We'd like to see him. When will you be home?"

"Probably around ten. Tom can walk me home. I'll have him come in, if it's not too late."

"We plan to listen to *The Shadow* tonight, so that's fine."

The two blocks seemed to fly under her feet. Even with the doubts in her head, the anticipation of being with Tom again exhilarated her. He stood on the porch as she came up the street but took the steps two at a time to join her when she started up the walk to the house. After a thorough hug and kiss, he exclaimed, "Pam, you look more and more beautiful every time I see you."

She giggled. "You just saw me a few hours ago."

He caressed her cheek. "Yes." His eyes glowed with a lovely fire, and she wanted to melt into his arms. "Come on, they're waiting for us." Tom offered his arm and they went into the house.

Tom's dad, Zeke, greeted them inside. "It's been awhile since we've seen you. Welcome back, Pam."

She smiled. "I know it must have been short notice. I hope I didn't put Mrs. Shafer out."

He shook his head. "We always have leftovers. There'll be enough. And Addy and I are delighted to have you here."

Addy put the last serving bowl on the table and put her hand on Pam's shoulder. "Sit down, dear, we're ready." Pam nodded to Emily and to Scott, Tom and Emily's fifteen-year-old brother, on the other side of the table. This put her back to the times in high school when she used to come here for dinner frequently. The pot roast and gravy smelled heavenly. She put an extra ladle of gravy on her mashed potatoes and dug in. Later, dessert was Addy's warm blueberry pie with a scoop of ice cream.

Pam sighed with a full stomach. "Thank you so much for the wonderful meal, Mrs. Shafer. I wish I could cook as well."

Addy grinned. "It just takes practice and a good teacher. I'm glad you enjoyed it."

"Here, let me help you clean up." Pam started to pick up the dishes.

Addy put her hand on Pam's arm. "No, Emily and Scott can help. You and Tom catch up."

Zeke turned on the radio in the living room as Tom guided Pam out to the porch. The wicker swing creaked and the springs squeaked as they sat together. The sun was still well up above the horizon, and the summer breeze caressed her face. Tom put his arm across her shoulders.

"There's something bothering you. I can see it in your face. What is it?" Tom's brown eyes burned into her own.

Pam sighed. "I guess I wonder if things have changed between us. I've written you so many letters in the past year, but you've only sent me six."

"I told you I don't get much time on my own. When the army grants me some free time, I usually sleep."

"Do you ever get lonely, Tom? I do. That's the reason I went to that dance. I couldn't take sitting at home another weekend." A sob escaped her lips.

Tom cupped her chin. "Yes, I get very lonely. I know my being away is hard on us, but I think there's something coming where my country will need me and others like me. Hank does, too. I have a bad feeling these battles around the world are going to suck us in. The Japanese are already making threats against us." He paused. "My feelings for you haven't changed. I love you." He kissed her deeply, and it curled her toes. She caressed his cheek where the late-day whiskers made it rough.

"I understand what you say, but it's so hard to be apart from the one you love."

He nodded. "Believe me, if the situation were different, I wouldn't leave your side."

"I know. So tell me, what is your life like in Anchorage?"

Tom smiled to himself. "Busy. The base still has a lot of construction to do, and the brass is under fire to get it done soon. I've helped on some of the work, but I also have aerial battle training to do at a moment's notice. The pilots have to drop everything and be ready to go up within five minutes."

They drifted from topic to topic, and Pam told him everything that had happened to their mutual friends. After they were talked out, the young couple sat for some time with their fingers interlaced, watching the sea fog make its way across the land, blocking out the sun.

Tom made a quick check of his watch. "It's a quarter to ten. Come on, I'll walk you home."

They stood, and the old springs squeaked again.

Pam shivered with the cool damp breeze. "I should've brought a wrap with me."

They went into the house, so she could thank and take her leave of the Shafers, and Tom picked up his army jacket. Outside, he put it around her shoulders. "That will keep you warm."

As they started on their way, Pam squeezed his hand. "Mother asked if you could stop in for a few minutes, before you start back."

He grinned. "Sure. I saw your father at the airfield when I came in, of course, but your mom and brother are pretty special, too."

When they arrived, Pam's mother greeted him with a kiss on the cheek. "It's good to see you, Tom. We have to have you over sometime this week."

Tom smiled. "Thank you, Mrs. Wright, I'll be happy to come."

Pam's kid brother was impressed with the army jacket. "Wow, it's made out of leather."

Tom removed it from Pam's shoulders and handed it to Ted to examine. "Yes, and it has a fleece lining. It can get cold up there in an airplane." When Ted returned it, Tom slipped it on. "I have to be getting back. It's good to see you all again."

Deep down, Pam was glad Tom and her family got along so well. Her father clapped Tom on the back. "We're proud of you and the other young men going into service in these dangerous times. Tell Hank and Joe, too."

"I will, sir. Joe wasn't able to get leave this time, but I'll tell him when I see him." Tom's half-Tlingit friend, Joe Nikoleavich, was in the navy with Hank. "Goodnight, all."

Pam came outside with him. He took her hand and touched her fingers one by one with his lips, before drawing her into a deep kiss that made her dizzy. "Sleep tight, sweetheart. Remember, I love you."

She nuzzled her face into the fleece that was exposed in the open jacket by his neck and breathed in his warm scent. "I love you, too." Her heart swelled as she watched him turn and put his hands in the pockets of his jacket. *I think I was foolish to believe he didn't care for me.* She could hear him whistling halfway down the block.

Chapter 2

Tom hauled the garbage out the restaurant door and down the steps to the big metal trash cans at the back of the building. He knew during this week he could relax, but it felt good to get back into the family business. As he lifted one of the lids and deposited the bundle into the can, he heard a snort behind him.

"Well, well, I knew I'd find the flyboy with the trash," Vic sneered. Tom noted the bruised nose and chin where he'd kneed him. *Doesn't this thug ever learn?*

"Don't you have anything better to do?"

"Not at the moment." Vic crossed his arms and leaned against the fence that shielded the refuse view from the building. "Pam had dinner with your family last night."

Tom pursed his lips and replaced the lid. "That's none of your business."

Vic straightened up and pointed at Tom. "Listen, you, I told you to stay away from her."

"And what are you going to do about it? I'm not the little kid you could beat up and steal money from in school. I know you're two years older, and heavier, but I showed you yesterday I can get back at you now. Pam can make up her own mind, so take a powder, Vic." Tom waved his hand like he was chasing a pesky fly.

Vic hesitated, as though he wanted to lunge at Tom, but he whirled away and stomped to the street. He turned to glare at Tom before he disappeared. Tom leaned against the fence, took a cigarette from a pack and lit it with his Zippo. A cloud of smoke drifted up as his cousin Jenny came around the fence.

She flashed her dark eyes at him. "What was that all about?"

Tom smiled. "The town bully isn't getting his way with me anymore and he's pi-, er, upset about it."

The corners of Jenny's mouth edged up. "You don't have to censor yourself around me. I'm a big girl now."

He swept her hand up and kissed it. "You're still a lady, I presume, and my elder."

She pulled her hand away and smacked him on the head. "You're insufferable." She marched back into the building.

Tom chuckled as he drew off the cigarette again. In a moment Hank joined him outside.

"Hey, Sis was complaining about you when she came in. What did you do?" Hank pointed at the cigarette. "Could I bum one of those off you?"

Tom shook one out of the pack and handed him the lighter. "I reminded her she was older than me."

"Since you brought the subject up, I was told by my mother that we're having Jenny's birthday celebration here at the restaurant Sunday evening. Of course, your family is invited. So is Pam."

Tom shook his head. "I have no idea what to get a twenty-year-old woman. Any thoughts on what she wants, or should I rely on my mother?"

"Emily might know. Those two confide in each other all the time." The two boys finished their cigarettes and headed inside.

Laden with the information from Em that Jen loved the fur-trimmed sweaters so in style, Tom went to the mercantile to check out the fall line. He found one in Jen's favorite green color and was soon headed to the theater with the package tucked under his arm. That was when he spotted the group of three, Vic and two of his cronies, a half-block away. A danger flare went off in Tom's brain, but before he could alter his route, he was seen. He considered turning and running, but he knew they would catch up, from this distance. Tom stood his ground and let them come to him.

"Hey, flyboy, out for a shopping trip?" Vic sneered.

"What do you want now? I'm getting fed up with you harassing me. Knock it off, Vic!"

Vic's two buddies moved on either side of Tom, who tried to skirt them, but Vic was in his way. The two grabbed Tom's arms, and the package dropped to the pavement. Vic retrieved it and opened the paper. "Well, isn't this a girly sweater for a flyboy!"

Tom struggled with the brutes as they pinned his arms behind his back. "Why can't this be between you and me? Afraid to face me alone?"

An ugly smile graced Vic's lips. "You have all the answers, don't you, *Tomas*? You can't even have the American name of Thomas. You have a goddamn spic name. That's because your mama is a spic, ain't she?"

"Fuck you, Vic! Leave my mother out of it!"

Vic slapped Tom. "And you have a damn Injin working for you. That's probably why the Injin section of the theater is as clean as the white section. Spic and Injin lovers!"

Tom spit in his face and Vic slammed his fist into Tom's gut. The air went out of his lungs and he collapsed to his knees. Before he could react, he heard a car stop and a door slam.

"What the hell is going on here?" The two thugs let go, and Tom heard them running down the street as he was helped to his feet. "Tom, can you stand?"

Tom took a couple of gasping breaths. "I think so." He looked into the face of Sheriff Sam Lindsey.

"Thank God you happened by."

Sam inclined his head in the direction the three disappeared. "What was that all about?"

Tom hesitated. "Vic wants to date Pam and keeps trying to pick a fight with me."

"Do you want to press charges?"

Tom picked up his parcel and inspected it. "No. This is between Vic and me." He replaced the paper and tucked the package under his arm.

"That's not wise, Tom. Vic and his friends aren't up to childish pranks. Someone, like you, could get hurt."

"It was lucky you happened by."

Sam waved his hand toward the beauty shop across the street. "Actually, Edna called me when she saw what was happening."

Tom looked over and there was his mother's beautician watching them. He gave her a salute. Tom turned back to the sheriff. "For now, I'll handle Vic on my own."

Sam studied him carefully. "Don't let it get out of hand. Come on. I'll give you a ride to the theater."

Tom felt the pain in his midsection and agreed to a lift. He settled in the passenger seat of the squad car and let out a shaky breath, suddenly exhausted.

Sam glanced over. "Maybe we should stop at the hospital first."

Tom shook his head. "No, I've had hits like this in basic training. I'd know if I was really hurt."

Sam smirked. "They toughen up the soldiers, eh?" He drove the car around to the back of the theater. "Tom, I think you should tell your family and your girlfriend what happened. A guy like Vic would think nothing of hurting any of them."

"Thanks for the lift, Sheriff, and the advice. I hadn't thought about him hurting anyone else."

Sam tipped his hat as Tom got out of the squad

car and went up the steps to the stage door. When he slid into the dressing room area, he found his mother conferring with their costume head, Kata Nikoleavich. It had never been of concern to him that this woman, his pal Joe's mother, was Tlingit, and he greeted her fondly. "I'm sorry Joe couldn't get leave with us, but he should be here in a week or so, according to Hank."

Kata gave him a warm smile. "It's not the same around here without you three getting in trouble. You boys sure kept it interesting."

Kata's sixteen-year-old daughter Marita came in with a pile of mending. "Hello, Tom. We've missed you around here." Her dark eyes sparkled with adoration.

"Helping your mother with the costuming now?"

"I've discovered I enjoy sewing, so I hope to work with her."

Tom took her hand and squeezed it. "You'll make some guy a good wife someday." He grinned as she blushed. He turned to his mother. "Can we talk?"

She nodded. "We can go to the old apartment."

Snaking their way through the theater, the restaurant and the office, they entered his parents' former apartment, now used for storage. His mother drew up two old wicker chairs and crossed her arms as she sat. "Edna called."

Tom flushed. "My, she was busy."

"Did you bring charges against Vic?"

"No, because this is between him and me. No real damage was done."

"Tom, he's been a bully all his life. I remember you coming home from school with cuts and bruises. If you aren't concerned about yourself, be concerned for Pam."

"I told her if anything happens she should go to either her family or ours."

His mother looked uncomfortable. "That may not be enough."

"Why?" *What can Mom know about it?*

A tear appeared in her eye. "Please don't ask me any more. Just don't let her get hurt in this vendetta of yours."

Tom sat back in the chair and handed her the package. "Could you wrap this for me? It's a present for Jenny."

She unwrapped it. "It has some dirt on it." She shook it out. "I can fix it up for you." She was silent for a moment. "Tom, think about what I said."

He stood and kissed her cheek. "I will, thank you, Mom." Leaving her, he saw his uncle going out the lobby door. "Uncle Josh, where's Dad?"

"He's setting up the new projector in the booth, with Ivan."

"Thanks!" Tom slipped through the open door to the small room that seemed even smaller with Kata's Russian husband filling it. While Tom's father finished bolting the projector to the floor, Tom greeted the large bearded man. "Hello, Ivan. Tell Joe, when you see him, I'm sorry I missed him this time."

Ivan grinned. "You can be sure I will."

Tom's dad stood and brushed off his knees. "Ivan, can you aim the light and set it? I want to talk to Tom."

Ivan nodded, and Tom and his dad sat on the stairs to the upper level. "Your mother told me what happened. You don't look worse for wear. Did you worm out of a fight?"

Tom took a deep breath and his stomach reminded him. "Not completely. His cronies held me while Vic punched me in the gut. When the sheriff stopped by, the cowards took off. Before you ask, no, I didn't bring charges."

"Why?"

"Because that won't make things any better. When he got out, he'd be even angrier at me. If I can show him I won't back down, he may get bored and move on."

"What about Pam? This whole thing seems to be over her. Don't forget she can be hurt, too."

Tom studied his father's face. "Mom said the same thing, and that it happened to her. She told me not to ask her any more. Was she ever attacked by a man?"

His father looked very sad at what must have been a memory he'd just as soon forget. "When she was in pictures, she had a bad experience with a co-star. Out of respect for her wishes, that's all I'll tell you."

Questions bubbled inside Tom's head as his father got up abruptly. "I've got things to do. Go help Hank set up the restaurant." And with that his father went back to the booth.

****

The morning rush was over at Millie's, and Pam sat at one of the empty tables with a steaming cup of coffee. The lunch crowd was an hour away, so she was taking a break with Millie's blessing. She needed to decide what to wear to Jenny's birthday party, for one thing. She took a look at the morning paper propped up on the napkin holder, and then an uneasy feeling made her turn around.

"Morning, Pam." Vic loomed over her.

"Hello, Vic." She turned back to the paper.

"I want to talk to you, honey." He sat across from her.

She shuddered, but kept her voice steady. "What do you want?"

Vic leaned toward her. "I wanted to let you know about your boyfriend's family. Did you know his mother is a spic?"

She pursed her lips. "A what?"

"A Mexican."

"Yes, I know Mrs. Shafer is half-Mexican. So?"

"Doesn't that bother you that she isn't a whole American?"

Pam put the newspaper down and glared at him. "What are you saying? Mrs. Shafer is as American as you or me."

"And they have a Tlingit woman for a seamstress."

"I know that, too. Mrs. Nikoleavich is very nice, and she's also an American, Vic."

He put his hand over one of hers. "Sweetheart, I have to school you about these inferiors."

She yanked her hand away and stood. "You can leave, Vic. You're giving the white race a bad name. And *don't* call me 'sweetheart.'"

It was his turn to glare. Then an ugly smile spread across his face. "One day, you'll know I was right. I hope it's before you decide who to marry. You don't want little brown babies."

"Get out, Vic!"

Millie looked up as Vic left. She came over to Pam. "I heard some of that. I was going to toss him out if he kept bothering you. Too many in this town have that attitude, but I've found it's easier to get to know a person before you condemn them."

Pam nodded. "That's what my father says, too. I've found good and bad in all groups."

Millie waved her hand toward the door. "And that one is as bad as they come. You must not have heard about the fight between Vic and Tom yesterday."

Pam stared at her. "No, I didn't. What happened?"

Millie related the fight on the street.

Pam hated that she had even spoken to Vic. "How is Tom? Do you know?"

"I heard from Edna that he was able to walk,

but the sheriff drove him to the theater."

Pam's dad picked her up that afternoon. In the car, he turned to her at a stop sign. "Tom came by earlier and said he would pick you up to take you to the theater around six."

She nodded. "Thank you, Dad. So he's all right." She hesitated a few moments, trying to decide if she should tell him about Vic. "Have you heard about Tom and Vic?"

He nodded. "It's all around town. Why didn't you tell me?"

"I didn't want to worry you. Besides, I didn't know about the fight yesterday until Millie told me, after Vic was in the restaurant this morning. He called Mrs. Shafer and Mrs. Nikoleavich 'inferiors.' I told him to leave."

"I don't know what to tell you about the intolerant people here, but there are a lot of them. Honey, all I can tell you is to stand up for what you believe in. Sometimes it goes against the majority."

Pam sighed. "I know, but everyone who knows the Shafers seems to like them."

"If you really love Tom, believe in him. I've known the Shafers for many years. They had a lot of ups and downs when they first came here, but they stood their ground. That's what brought many to their side. Now, they're considered a solid part of the community."

Pam thought about all that as she got ready for the party. Tom had been such a tease when they were in grammar school, but she fell in love with the dark-haired, brown-eyed heartbreaker in high school. Every time she thought of him, she smiled. She couldn't help herself.

Hearing the Ford station wagon pull into the driveway sent Pam to her upstairs window. As Tom got out, she grabbed the cardigan sweater that matched her powder-blue sleeveless party dress, gave her lips a quick swipe with her lipstick, and tucked that and her compact into her purse.

Tom was waiting downstairs and gave her a wide grin as she came into the hallway. "You look beautiful tonight."

She gave him a hug, then picked up the present for Jenny and waved to her parents in the living room. "I'm going."

Her mother glanced up. "When are you going to be home?"

Tom put his arm around Pam. "I'll have her home around midnight."

"Wish Jenny a happy birthday for us."

Her father put down his newspaper. "Tom, you and Pam be careful, since you've had the trouble with Vic."

Tom nodded. "Don't worry, Mr. Wright, I'll take care of Pam."

At the station wagon, Tom helped Pam in and then settled himself in the driver's seat.

As he turned into the road, Pam sighed. "Tom, I heard about the fight with Vic yesterday." She told him about Vic's visit at Millie's.

Tom frowned. "Maybe everyone was right. I should have brought charges against him."

Suddenly, Pam shivered. "I want him to stay away from both of us. I can't take this—" She started to cry.

Tom stopped the station wagon in front of the theater and put his arms around her, holding her tight. "I wish I didn't have to go back in two days."

Pam clung to him. She wanted to be encased in this cocoon forever, but after a few moments she dried her face. "Let's go in." As he got out and came around to the passenger door, she quickly repaired her makeup with the compact and lipstick.

He helped her out and put his arms around her again. "Are you sure you're all right?"

Pam nodded and retrieved the present from the front seat. "I shouldn't let Vic get to me like that, but he doesn't seem to take the hint." She took a deep breath, arranged her face into what she hoped was a happy expression, and took Tom's hand.

Once they were through the lobby doors and into the restaurant, Pam sought out Jenny to give her the gift, and Jenny put it on the package table and hugged her. "I'm glad you could come. I've missed you and Tom at the restaurant. Come over and visit more often."

"I felt funny coming here to visit by myself."

Jenny shook her head. "Don't. You're practically family."

A warm glow traveled through her. "Thank you, I will."

Pam found Tom talking with his uncle James, Hank's kid brother Don, and Scott. James grinned as she slipped to Tom's side. "Hello, Pam. I'm sorry I haven't been to Millie's lately, but we just got our new tower at the station, and I had to supervise its installation."

"I think of the three radio stations in Juneau, yours is the best."

His eyes sparkled with pride. "We try to get the best programs. Now I have to get these two kids to learn how to do the lighting and sound in the theater, since I've put in new equipment here."

Noticing Tom's mother and two aunts were starting to set up the table, Pam put a hand on Tom's shoulder. "I'm going to help them set up."

Tom kissed her cheek. "See you in a few minutes."

Muriel directed Pam to help Emily, who was doing place settings and handed Pam the silverware case. "I hate this job," Emily said as she put the plates and glasses around.

Just as Pam was finishing, Jenny came over

with a young man. "Chase, I want you to meet Tom's girlfriend, Pam Wright. Pam, this is Chase Marshall, my intended."

Pam studied his face. "I've seen you in Millie's before. I work there."

His green eyes shone as he smiled. "Yes, I thought I recognized you, too. You're the daughter of Bill Wright, at the airfield, aren't you? I work as a postal clerk in town."

"So you must have seen Dad many times. The best wishes to both of you in your upcoming marriage."

Jenny leaned toward Pam. "Could you be one of my bridesmaids?"

"Thank you for asking me. When is the wedding?"

"Next June, so we have plenty of time."

Pam nodded. "Wonderful. I'll be happy to."

Everyone gathered around the table as Amelia brought out the crown roast of pork, complete with gold paper on top. James kissed her cheek. "It looks like you've done yourself proud again, my love."

She blushed and looked down quickly. Her "Thank you" was almost inaudible.

Pam found herself seated between Tom and Emily. Jenny was in the chair of honor at the head of the table, with Chase and Tom next to her. Tom's Uncle Josh had filled all the wine glasses before they sat down and now stood at the end of the table with his glass raised in a toast. "Here's to our dear Jenny. She's done an excellent job of running the restaurant since Cora left. Now our sweet girl is all grown up and ready to settle down. You are a joy to your mother and me. Many years of happiness we wish to you."

They all raised their glasses toward her and said, "Hear, hear!"

As they dug into their meal, Pam heard Chase

ask Jenny, "Have you any idea who will take over the restaurant for you when we get married?"

Jenny hesitated for a moment. "I was going to continue running the restaurant."

"But, my dear, you need to take care of our home."

"I can do both. I'll take care of the house in the morning and work here in the afternoon."

Chase stared at her. "What about my dinner?"

"You could eat here with me."

He wiped his mouth with the napkin. "When we have a family, you have to stay home."

Jenny gave him a determined face. "My parents didn't bring this up, so I thought it was all right to continue working here. All of us were raised here, and I think we turned out all right. Don't you agree, Tom?"

Tom glanced at Jenny, as if reluctant to get into this. "Well, our parents were all here, so I think that was different."

Chase shook his head. "I'll let you continue here until we have a family, but after that, you will stay home."

Jenny gazed at her plate and didn't say anything more.

Pam was shocked with Jenny's resolve to work after she was married. It just wasn't done, unless a woman worked with her husband or they needed the extra income. Her own mother had worked as a secretary for a year or so during the tough times a few years ago, to make ends meet, but she quit after Pam's father got his job at the airfield. Pam had hated it when she came home from school and her mother wasn't there. A mother belonged in the home.

Jenny brought Pam out of her reverie. "Pam, would you like to go to work for me? One of the waitresses is leaving, and I know you're good."

"Will you let me think about it? I'll give you an answer in a day or so. Anyway, I'd have to give notice to Millie." Millie was a good friend, and Pam enjoyed working for her, but the idea of working with Tom's family gave her comfort. She would feel closer to him.

Emily bumped Pam with her elbow. "Oh, do! That'll be fun, to have you here."

Pam noticed that Hank, seated next to Chase across from them, was uncharacteristically quiet. She leaned over to Tom. "What's wrong with Hank?"

Tom glanced at him and turned to her. "His girl, Mary Jean, threw him over for another guy. Seems she didn't like having him gone most of the time."

I can sympathize with her, but I won't tell Tom that. Sadness wafted over her. She didn't want to think about Tom leaving again for who knew how long.

Amelia had disappeared and now returned with a beautiful layer cake. The icing was white with green trim along the top and bottom edges, topped by a large red rose. Twenty candles shimmered on it, and everyone sang "Happy Birthday" as Jenny blew out the candles.

Pam watched Jenny cut the cake. *I have a feeling I know what her wish was. She's too determined to run the restaurant.*

Before long, Josh brought out the portable turntable and a folder of records. "A little dancing will settle the dinner." He laughed, and his wife, Muriel, sparkled back at him.

Tom turned to take Pam by the arm, but she shook her head. "I'm going to dance with Hank first. He needs some cheering up."

Tom pursed his lips. "Okay, but I get the next one."

She kissed his cheek and made her way over to Hank. Putting her hand on his shoulder, she declared, "Girl's choice."

Hank looked up in surprise. "Tom told you, didn't he?"

"I tortured it out of him. You need to smile again." Strains of "I Want to be Happy" echoed across the room. "Perfect selection," Pam said as she pulled him up.

As they stepped out onto the dance floor, Pam laughed. "Mary Jean is a dope to throw over a dreamboat like you. You'll have plenty of girls to replace her."

His hazel eyes crinkled at the corners. "Can you be one?"

"If it wasn't for Tom, I'd be yours in a minute."

He whirled her around. "Then I'll have to get rid of him."

At the end of the song, she cupped his face. "Seriously, if you ever need anyone to talk or write to, I'll listen or write back."

Hank kissed her. "Thank you, Pam. I will."

Tom pushed them apart. "That's enough of that."

Hank cocked his eyebrow. "Jealous?"

Tom ignored him and steered Pam to the center of the room. The song "Deep Purple" found them holding each other tight. "You seem to have perked him up. What did you say to him?" he whispered in her ear.

She nuzzled his neck. "That there were many girls who would love to be with him. And if he wanted to talk or write about something, I would be there for him."

He pulled back and gazed at her. "As long as you're there for me, too."

Her heart swelled and her eyes misted over. "You know I will be." She thought of how soon he would have to leave, and the tears overflowed.

They stopped dancing as he stroked her cheek.

"Here now, what's wrong?"

She threw her arms around his shoulders. "It's so hard to see you go."

He hugged her back. "You still have me now. Let's enjoy the time we have left, and I promise to write more." They danced again.

Too soon, the party was over. Pam squeezed into the back of the station wagon between Tom and Emily, with Scott between his parents in the front. When Zeke pulled into their driveway, he flipped the keys back to Tom. "So you can take Pam home."

As the rest of the family disappeared into the house, Pam and Tom settled into the front seat. Tom parked outside her home with the radio in the dash emitting the sweet sounds of "Moonlight Serenade." Pam closed her eyes. "This reminds me of the many dates we had in high school. I thought I had found my white knight."

He put his arm around her. "I know I found my lady." He looked at his watch. "We have a few minutes yet." Tom turned and locked his lips to hers.

Slipping her hand inside his jacket, she felt the warmth of his shirt, and he gave a deep moan and shifted. Her fingertips brushed the taut muscles of his chest as they rippled under the cloth. When he ran a trail of kisses down her throat to the hollow of her collarbone, it was her turn for a moan to rumble deep in her chest.

Suddenly, Tom stopped. "Uh-oh," he said and nodded toward the house. There was her father, watching from the porch like he used to, the smoke from his pipe curling in the night air. They glanced at each other, disheveled and gasping, then laughed. "Caught again." Tom smirked. Her father waved at them both.

Pam was very close to wanting to kill her father, but she took a shaky breath. "Do you want me to walk in front of you up to the house?"

Tom sighed. "This is too much like it used to be." He got out and opened the passenger door, maneuvering behind Pam after he helped her out. "Good evening, Mr. Wright," he said as they stood at the bottom of the steps.

Her father raised one eyebrow. "Come in for a few minutes, Tom?"

"Oh, no, thank you, sir. I've got to be getting back."

He smiled. "Remember, Tom, you can't pull anything a girl's father doesn't already know about."

Pam cleared her throat. "Can I at least kiss Tom goodnight without an audience?"

Her father looked at his watch. "Two minutes." He went inside.

Pam turned into welcoming arms and held Tom tight for a deep and satisfying goodnight kiss. Tom pushed up hard against her pelvis. "Someday, my love, someday." Pam felt her body respond with intense tingling.

She grasped the handrail to the porch to steady herself as he went back to the station wagon. She was breathing heavily, and she hadn't even gone up the steps yet.

Chapter 3

Tom sat, his arm around Pam, with friends and the non-acting members of his family, watching the dress rehearsal for *Gold Rush*, the musical his dad and Uncle Josh had written. In the role of Yukon Lil was his sister, Emily, who was now official understudy to her mother, and she was singing the tender love song "You and the Alaskan Moon" with Lil's love, Ike, being played by her father.

Jen, on the other side of Tom, dug an elbow into his ribs. "Em does very well, but there's something very strange in having her father play her lover. In this case one of the other boys in the cast should play the other lead, don't you think?"

Tom hadn't thought of that and wished Jen hadn't, either, because suddenly it struck him funny. Hank must have overheard, because he turned around in the seat in front of them, adding to the laughter. That completely threw off everyone on stage. In seconds, the whole row of family audience was engulfed in gales of glee.

Dan Hanson stood from his place in the audience. "May I remind the spectators that this isn't one of the humorous sections of the play?"

Tom's dad stalked to the edge of the stage. "Okay, which one of you hooligans started this?"

As one, they all pointed at Jenny. She looked around at the others and said, "Uh—"

Hank piped up and repeated what she'd said, and she batted him on the back of his head.

Tom's dad paused a moment. "Maybe we should do a rehearsal with the understudies." He pointed to one of the boys with a minor part. "Dave, you've been in the cast from the start. Do you think you can handle the lead?"

Dave Kendall nodded. "Yes, sir."

"Then I'll take your part for a while. We'll lay my niece's incestuous thoughts to rest. What do you think, Dan?"

Hanson was silent for a moment. "I think that's a good idea. Places, everyone! We'll take this from the beginning of the scene."

At the end of the play, the dutiful audience gave the cast a standing ovation. "Author, author!" they all cried.

Zeke and his brother Josh came to the front of the stage and took a bow. Later, backstage, Tom put his arms around both his dad and his uncle. "Hey, you two, that was one of the best musicals I've seen. In fact, I don't think I've seen better on screen."

Uncle Josh grinned. "You're not just saying that because we're family?"

Hank laughed. "You know Tom would tell you if it stunk. I'm impressed, too." He waved his hand toward them. "Presenting the next Rodgers and Hart!"

Tom's dad handed over the keys to the station wagon. "Here, Tom, you can take Pam home, but remember to come back for us."

Tom raised an eyebrow. "Don't I always?"

"Get going!"

Tom clasped Pam's hand, and they went out to the car. When they got to the Wrights', Pam's smile melted and she snuggled into his waiting arms. "You're leaving tomorrow, and I can't stand it. When will I see you again?"

He stroked her hair. "We usually get leave every six months now, but I'm going to see if I can delay it until June, so I can be here for Jen's wedding."

"But that's almost a year." She moaned into his

shoulder.

He pulled back and cupped her chin, wiping the tears with his other hand. "I'll write often, now that I know how much it means to you. I love you."

She opened her purse and drew out a small picture of herself that looked like it had been taken at the drugstore's photo booth. She slipped it into his shirt pocket. "Keep this close to your heart. Know that I love you."

Looking deep into her eyes, he felt his heart breaking. "I leave from the airfield at ten tomorrow morning. You'll be there?"

She nodded. "I'll go in with my father. I've already asked Millie for the morning off." They shared one more prolonged kiss before he walked her to the door. As he started the engine, he looked back at the Wrights' house. *I wish I could be sure Pam is going to be safe. This whole thing with Vic worries me. But what can I do? I've already signed on to protect the country.*

Tom went back to the theater and drove the rest of his family home. It was his last night there, and he sat with his parents at the kitchen table for some time after Scott and Emily had said their goodnights.

"Dad, do you know where Vic works? I want to talk to him before I leave."

His mother shook her head. "After what he did to you the last time, why do you want to seek him out?"

"I don't want to fight him. I want to reach an understanding. I don't like to leave things hanging, especially where Pam is concerned."

His dad's expression was troubled. "Vic works as a mechanic at the service station down the block from the theater. I need gas for the station wagon, so we can stop there tomorrow morning."

"Zeke?" Tom's mother looked worried.

His dad put his hand over hers. "Addy, Tom's right. He can't ignore this."

Tom rose. "Thanks, Dad." Tom kissed his mother on the cheek. "I'll be all right, Mom. I think I'll turn in now. Goodnight." He hoped he sounded calmer than he felt.

The next morning, Tom took leave of his kid brother and Emily before hopping into the station wagon with his parents. When they arrived at the theater, his uncle and aunt were out in front with Hank and Jenny. Tom hurried out of the car. "I'm glad I caught you in time!" He gave his cousin a bear hug. "Take care of yourself, you old seadog!"

Grinning, Hank shook Tom's shoulders. "You're older than I am, you army Rat!"

Hank said goodbye to Tom's parents while Tom did the same with his aunt and uncle and Jenny.

After Dad dropped Mom at the theater, he and Tom headed to the service station. His dad didn't say anything until they glanced at each other as Tom opened the door to get out. "Be careful, son."

Tom passed the smiling station attendant, on his way to pump the gas and talk to Dad, and with a deep breath continued on into the car repair bays. One of the workers, a man he knew as Jake, looked up with a smile. "Can I help you?"

"Will you tell me where Vic Houston is?"

Jake nodded toward an old blue Oldsmobile. "He's working under the hood over there."

"Thanks, Jake." The smell of gas, grease, and rubber hit Tom's nose as he made his way to the Olds. He saw Vic with a wrench, tightening something in the engine. Tom leaned against the fender. "Vic, do you have a moment?"

Vic looked surprised, and Tom noticed his grease-grimed hand clench the wrench tighter. "What do you want, Shafer?" His voice was rough.

"I didn't come here to fight you, but before I

leave to go back to base, I have something to say. If I hear you've hurt Pam in any way, I will find you and you will be sorry."

Vic's fingers bunched the dirty cloth that covered the radiator grill. "I don't plan to hurt Pam, but that doesn't mean I won't try to date her. And the big-time flyboy didn't bring any charges against me. Are you too chicken?" He spit on the floor by Tom's feet.

Tom's temper flared, but he held it in check. "She has told you she has no interest in you. I know family and friends around her will be watching you. I want you to stop harassing her."

"We'll see about that. I have friends, too, got that?"

"I consider this between you and me. Remember what I said, Vic. I'm not scared of you." Tom turned and departed from the repair bays. He slid into the passenger side of the station wagon as the attendant was collecting payment for the gas.

His dad turned to him. "How did it go?"

"I think he was surprised I showed up here, but I delivered my message, and I'm still in one piece."

His dad snorted. "That's saying something." At the theater, his mother was waiting, and Tom jumped out of the front to settle in the back seat next to his duffel bag as she climbed in.

His mother turned around. "How did it go with Vic?"

Pursing his lips, Tom said briefly, "I told him to stay away from Pam."

She sighed. "That's all you're going to tell me?"

"Yep." He stared out the window the rest of the way.

****

Pam anxiously glanced at the clock. The army mail plane was warming up while the pilot finished loading it. Her father put his hand on her shoulder.

"Don't worry, they still have ten minutes."

As soon as she saw the Ford station wagon coming up the drive, she shot out of the mail office, and Tom was in her arms in seconds. She rubbed her fingers inside his unzipped jacket to feel the small square photo in his shirt pocket, and he put his hand over hers. "And there it will stay," he promised.

Tears overwhelmed her eyes as he kissed her.

He pulled back and wiped her cheeks. "Here now, smile for me, love."

Pam attempted to. "Please remember to write. Getting your letters will make me less lonely. Tell me what you're doing, and I will write as often."

Tom wordlessly drew her into a hug. Then he said his goodbyes to his parents. His mother, distraught, was held tightly by his father, who gave Tom a firm handshake and a quick, "Take care, son." When Pam's father appeared beside Pam, Tom shook his hand, as well. "Take care of her."

"I will. God speed, Tom."

Tom kissed Pam again, then climbed into the airplane. She couldn't help it. Sobs broke from her, and she felt her father's arm go around her. He handed her his handkerchief, and she mopped her eyes to watch as the airplane bumped along the ground, then rose to glide into the cloudy skies, disappearing swiftly.

As her vision dimmed with tears again, she heard Mr. and Mrs. Shafer come up beside them and saw Zeke put his hand on her father's shoulder. "We can take Pam back to town, if you'd like."

Her father nodded. "Thank you, Zeke. You'll have to come over and visit more. We've lost touch since Tom has been gone."

Zeke grinned. "We will. And you're welcome to our house, as well, remember."

Addy pulled herself together and took Pam's arm. "Come on, dear. Keeping busy is going to take our minds off Tom. At least for a while."

Pam kissed her father on the cheek. "I'll see you after work."

He waved as she climbed into the back seat of the station wagon, still warm from where Tom had been. She leaned toward the window, gazing at the direction Tom's airplane had taken. Another wave of loneliness and sadness surged over her.

Addy turned to her. "Have you given Millie notice yet? Jen wanted me to ask you."

Pam nodded. "Yes, I'll be starting at the Golden North Restaurant in two weeks, if that's all right."

"Did Millie mind? She won't come up short, will she?"

"No. She said she understood and wished me well, and she has in mind another girl she thinks will pick up the job quickly."

Addy was silent for a moment. "Pam, anytime you're feeling blue about Tom not being here, come talk to me. I'll be missing him, too."

Pam moved up on the seat and put a hand on Addy's shoulder. "Thank you. I will."

Addy reached up and put her fingers on Pam's and gave them a squeeze. "This is hard on all of us."

When they arrived at Millie's, well before the lunchtime rush, Zeke opened the car door and helped Pam out, accepting her thanks with a warm smile and a quick pat on the shoulder.

Inside, Millie motioned to Pam from behind the counter.

"Pam, Vic was looking for you earlier. I didn't tell him where you were, just that you took the morning off."

Her stomach knotted. "Did he say why?"

"No. He walked out after that." Millie nervously rubbed her hand on the apron. "If he comes back this afternoon, stay in the restaurant area so I can watch. I don't trust him."

"Don't worry. I'm not going anywhere with him."

After the busy midday, Pam took some coffee to a table for a break. With stationery borrowed from Millie, she had just started a letter to Tom when Vic appeared and stood across from her. Indicating a chair, he said, "May I?"

Pushing down her fear and anger, she tried to look indifferent. "No. I have nothing to say to you." She snuck a peek at the counter, where Millie was busy wiping the already shining surface.

He gripped the back of the seat. "I want to say I'm sorry for what I've been doing to you and Tom."

Surprise and suspicion traveled through her mind. "What brought this on?"

He gazed at the tabletop, then back at her. "Pam, I don't know how to treat anyone, so I take what I want." He paused. "My father hightailed it out of town when I was three, and my mother is a drunk. I don't know them social graces."

She watched him carefully. Was he telling the truth or manipulating her? "Why are you telling me this?"

"Because when I saw you at that party, I wanted you to be my girl. No other girl had ever been nice to me. Pam, I've been lonely."

Part of her hurt for him. "You'll never win anyone with anger. People are scared or repulsed by it. If you want people to be nice to you, you have to be nice to them."

He gazed steadily at her. "Can I be nice to you?"

Something in his eyes made her uncomfortable. "I have to tell you, I'm loyal to Tom. He's always been good to me and treats me like a lady. To use your words, I'm his girl."

A shadow crossed his eyes, then he turned toward the door, saying, "Girls like to be fought over." He walked out of the restaurant.

Chapter 4

Dear Sweetheart,

It's very cold and dark, and the storms seem to never end. It's hard to fly in this weather, but I guess we have to be ready for anything. The way the President has been helping Churchill might bring down the wrath of the Germans on us. Everyone's waiting for the other shoe to drop.

I miss you more than you will ever know. Now that the Holiday season is coming, I wish I could be at home with you. Here in Anchorage, the lights are all up in the downtown, and I miss all the shopping trips we used to do in Juneau.

Well, say a prayer for me tonight, and I hope our country comes out of this without going into war, but you never know.

All my love,

Tom

The Alaskan evening wind howled around the junior officer's Quonset hut. Tom finished his letter to Pam, then set it on the nightstand next to his bed. He would post it in the morning. Kicking off his boots, he swung his legs onto the bed and lay back. This early in December, and he was already thinking about Christmas, especially since the dark this time of year was depressing.

"Hey, Tom! You didn't show up in the O Club tonight. Feelin' poorly?" One of his three roommates, Ken Edwards, an endlessly cheerful Texan, strode into their quarters.

"No, just finishing a letter to my girl. The flying was hell today, wasn't it?"

"Goddamn plane kicked like an unbroken colt in this weather. This makes a Texas twister feel like a Sunday-go-to-meetin' breeze." Plopping on his bed across from Tom, Ken continued, "How can you stand living up here?"

"Never lived anywhere else. Except Seattle, for basic."

"Stan and Ernie back yet?"

"Nope. Quiet as a tomb in here." Suddenly a door slammed. "Speak of the devil—"

The two missing cohorts reeled in, drunk as a couple of skunks, leaning on each other as if each had only one leg. Stan Lobowski's blond hair hung in stringy locks over his eyes, and Ernie Kelly's clothes were in impossible disarray. When Ernie jettisoned himself from Stan and fell across Ken's bed, Ken immediately dumped him onto the floor. "Whew, you smell like a pig barn in summer. Get to your own bed!"

The sots crawled to their beds, flopped face down, and passed out. Tiptoeing to the window on their side of the room, Tom cracked it open. "It may be colder in here, but at least we can breathe."

Ken shook his head. "It's a good thing tomorrow's Sunday. I wouldn't want one of those in an airplane in the morning."

The next day, Tom and Ken left the two laundry piles to sleep it off in bed and headed to the chaplain's hut for the Sunday service. On the way, Tom deposited his letter to Pam in the mailbox. After compulsory God, they followed their noses to the officer's mess.

Stan and Ernie were there, looking pitiful. Captain Allison, the squadron head, must have poured them out of bed. The captain gave Tom and Ken a wave over. "Why didn't you do something with your bunkmates this morning?"

Ken made a face. "I didn't think we had to be

nursemaids, sir."

"Always look after the other men, lieutenants. In a war, we have to watch out for each other. Understood?"

The boys stood at attention and saluted. "Yes, sir."

"Good. Go to breakfast."

Picking up their food from the cafeteria-style counters, Tom and Ken sat across from Stan and Ernie, who were nursing a cup of black coffee apiece. Tom blew some of the steam off his bacon and eggs, laughing as the hangover twins turned a delightful shade of green.

Suddenly, a grim-faced General Buckner strode into the officer's mess. Everyone stood at attention. "At ease. I have news." He gazed out at all the men, seeming to look each straight in the eye to judge their mettle before he continued. "What we feared the most has just happened. The Japs have bombed our navy battleships and Hickum Field at Pearl Harbor. The President will probably declare war before the day is out. All of you will get orders on where we will be sending you tomorrow. We need defenses on the Aleutians and have been building installations for the last month to help defend the naval installation at Dutch Harbor. Be ready to move at eleven hundred in the morning. That's first light." He left the stunned officers staring.

Tom's stomach knotted, and he took a glance at Ken, who was suddenly speechless and as pale as the two sots. "My dear God," was all Tom could say. *Well, this is what I've been training for.* All of a sudden, the United States was at war. Deep down, part of him had thought—had hoped—this would never come.

With flashing eyes, Ken looked at Tom. "Damn Japs! Who do they think they're playing with? Why don't they stay on their own goddamn island?"

Tom felt a surge through him. "We'll give them a fight, by God! They'll be sorry they ever tried to start something with Uncle Sam."

Their orders came after lunch. Tom and Ken were assigned to the secret air installation on Umnak Island, while Stan and Ernie were off to the airfield at Unalaska.

That evening, the four young lieutenants set up a poker game in their quarters. The air was heavy with tobacco smoke as they tried to take their minds off what lay ahead, but they played in unaccustomed silence.

Finally Stan piped up. "What do you think it will be like? I know we've trained for months for this and had mock air battles, but now we're going to be against people who want to kill us."

Ken laid down his cards. "Boy, remember the Japs will be thinkin' the same thing. I ain't going to lay down and let them stampede over me. Anyway, we're fresher than they are."

And they're more experienced, Tom added in his head. The somber faces of his companions told him they probably all thought that.

At oh-six-hundred hours, the boys were up and packing their duffel bags for the move, and in the few hours before departure time they ate breakfast and attended the necessary briefing meetings. Tom and Ken, assigned to Captain Allison's squad on their way to Umnak, said their goodbyes and Godspeeds to Stan and Ernie. The uncertainty of ever seeing any of them again weighed on Tom's mind.

At eleven hundred hours, the sun broke over the mountain range behind Anchorage, clear and cold, as the boys warmed up their P-40s to shake the chill of the night out of the engines. Tom double-checked his navigation charts and waited while several scout planes flew out ahead of them to make sure the area was clear. Then, at the signal, he took off.

Tom knew they were to maintain radio silence so as not to alert the Japanese. Ken was his wingman, and they had worked out a set of gestures for communication while they were in flight. Ken waved as he pulled up beside Tom.

Soon, the chain of islands spread out before them, with spotty fog fighting the bright sunshine sparkling off the sea water, sluggish with cold. Tom made a sign to Ken and pointed downward. There, coming up, was the naval installation at Dutch Harbor. The next island was Umnak, and they could see its large dormant volcano in the distance. The secret airfield in back of a cannery front was a grassy runway; the base was still unfinished.

The support crews, mechanics, cooks, office personnel, and all the others, had come by transport a few hours ahead of the pilots. Tom landed on the field, bouncing on the uneven ground in the cold December wind. After their two-and-a-half-hour flight, the short winter day was already in twilight as they turned the planes toward the large building still under construction.

Captain Allison called the pilots over when they were on the ground. "The colonel wants to brief all of you at oh-seven-hundred hours tomorrow. Meanwhile, we have some shacks ready, since the quarters in the building aren't finished yet. Settle in there, then come to the officers' mess in the main hall in the office section that's finished. There are eight beds in each shack. They have heat and electricity." He then read off who was assigned to each shack.

Both Tom and Ken ended up in shack number three. Tom shouldered his duffel bag and prepared to make the drafty temporary barracks his home. Like everything else the army had hastily put together, conditions weren't perfect: the lights faded and flickered whenever a gust of wind hit. The heater did keep the temperature warmer than the outdoors, but Tom could still see his breath.

He and Ken took two beds in the center, close to the heater, and after mess they crawled into their beds fully clothed, trying to keep from freezing. Tom dreamed warm visions of Pam.

****

Dear Pam,

You will be startled to get another letter from me so soon, but, as I'm sure you know by now, the Japs bombed Pearl Harbor. We flew out of Anchorage and I can't tell you where we went. I'll keep you informed if I have to go into combat, which my Commanding Officer is sure we will.

I've let my family know what is happening, as well. I realize you are working at the Golden North restaurant now. Tell Jen I may not be able to be there for her wedding. It depends how long this war goes on. I'm afraid it might be a long one.

My dear sweet girl, this is what I was talking about when I was home. I long to be with you and hold you in my arms, which I do in my dreams. If you get lonely, remember I'll always love you. Even though we're apart, you're still next to my heart and will stay there. Let's pray this action won't last real long and I'll be on the first flight home.

Until then, be brave, sweetheart, and ask God for my deliverance.

All my love,

Tom

Pam folded the letter and put it in the envelope, tucking it into her dresser drawer next to the others. Thinking back on that Sunday last week made her shudder. Her family had heard the horrible news after they returned from church. And now Tom was going into God only knew what kind of action against the enemy. She sent up a silent prayer for him.

She finished getting ready for work. Wednesday was usually a light day at the theater and restaurant, so she went in mid-afternoon. With the dark already overtaking the town, she rode with Mr. and Mrs. Shafer.

Climbing into the back of the station wagon, she sighed. "I received a letter from Tom this afternoon."

Addy nodded. "We did, too. He told us he was shipped out to another place."

They continued in silence to the theater. Pam tried not to think of the worst, but she knew this war would probably be one of the hardest things he would have to go through. *Well, if there's a way to send Tom some of my strength, I will.*

Two other waitresses were there, getting ready for the few moviegoers who wanted to escape the world for a while. They usually had about seven steady customers midweek.

Since there wasn't a lot for her to do, Pam checked on Amelia Carter in the kitchen. "Is there anything I can help you with?"

Amelia pointed to a bundle on the floor by the outside door. "That needs to be taken out to the trash can."

Pam took it out. As she replaced the lid on the can, she heard, "Can I talk to you?"

She whirled, and there was Vic, standing by the fence. Pam took a deep breath. "Make it fast. I'm busy."

He took a step toward her, but she kept her distance by taking a step back. "I wanted to tell you I enlisted in the army."

Part of her was relieved to get rid of him. "Good for you, Vic."

"You seem to like men in uniform."

"Don't push it. Let's be civil to each other, and I can wish you well."

"I'll make you proud of me, darlin'. You may give a hero a chance."

"Godspeed, Vic." She turned and walked inside.

Jenny was in the kitchen when Pam returned. She studied Pam's face. "What's wrong? You look pale."

"I ran into Vic outside. He made a point of telling me he's enlisted in the army."

"Do you need Dad or Uncle Zeke to run him off?"

"No, I think he's gone." She looked at the door behind her. "I hope."

Jenny looked concerned. "Why do you keep talking to him? I would tell him to go to heck."

"I'm more afraid of getting him angry. But I'm not encouraging him, either."

Pam was grateful for the customers who came in that evening. She could put her mind on serving them rather than worrying about her troubles.

Chase arrived during the evening, drawing Jenny to the back of the restaurant to talk with her. After Jenny cried out at one point, she and Chase went into the office.

When Jenny came back, Pam took her aside. "Is everything all right?"

Jenny glanced at her and then away sadly. "Something's come up about the wedding. I'll tell you after I discuss it with my parents tonight."

Jenny finished the night without a word and went home with her parents, while Pam accepted the offer of a ride from Zeke and Addy. When Pam settled in the back seat, Addy turned around. "I heard about Vic stopping over tonight. Are you all right?"

Pam sighed. "He told me he enlisted in the army. Truth be told, I'm glad to be rid of him."

Zeke spoke up. "I think you should talk to your father about taking legal action to keep him away from you. You can't let him keep bothering you like that."

"I feel sorry for him, in a way. He said his father abandoned him when he was three and his mother is a drunk."

Zeke glanced at his wife. "Pam," he said, "when Tom was in high school, I had many meetings with Vic's parents. He must have lied to make you feel sorry for him."

Pam's breath caught. She felt stupid and scared at the same time. "Tom told me about his encounters with Vic while he was in school. He never said you had met with Vic's parents."

"We didn't tell Tom about it. He probably would have been embarrassed to know that, back then."

Pam was struck dumb. She felt used. Vic had manipulated her feelings and hurt Tom. Did he really enlist, or was this another way to get to her? What more reason did she need to turn him away if he even tried to talk to her again? Her spine stiffened with resolve, and she swallowed hard. "Thank you for telling me this."

Addy shook her head. "You're young. Like you, I was raised to be nice and respectful of people, but I learned some don't deserve it. You have to find out who is who before anything unfortunate happens."

Stopping the station wagon in front of Pam's house, Zeke turned to her. "Talk to your father about this and see what he says."

Pam put a hand on his shoulder. "Thank you both, I will. Goodnight."

She waved to them from the front door and went in to find her parents listening to dance music on the radio in the living room. Strains of "Always" came drifting to her, and she thought of the times Tom had danced with her to that. She sat on the arm of the sofa.

Her mother looked up from her embroidery. "How was work, dear?"

Pam glanced at her hands. "Work was fine. Dad, Mom, I have to talk to you about Vic." She related what had happened that evening and what the Shafers had told her. "I don't know what to do. I want him to stop bothering me, and I don't want him to hurt Tom again."

Her father took a draw off his pipe. "Well, with him going into the army, he won't be around here much longer. In the meantime, never go anywhere without someone with you."

Her mother chewed her lip. "Do you think that will be enough?"

"Unless he starts getting violent, that should be. Judging from what's happening, he wants Pam to like him, so I don't believe he'll try to hurt her."

Pam didn't feel any easier, but she bid her parents goodnight and headed upstairs to bed. *How I wish Tom weren't so far away. I don't want to worry him with this, since he has so much more that concerns him.* Before she slept, she prayed for him and all who were in harm's way.

The next day, Pam went in early to help set up for the Juneau Rotary Club's Christmas party, to be held at the Golden North Restaurant. Although the country was at war, the government wanted the citizens to carry on as normally as possible.

As she was going into the theater, something caught her eye, a movement from the far corner of the building. The hairs on the back of her neck went up. *Something is wrong, I can feel it.* But she shrugged and opened the door, dismissing the feeling as silly.

But as Pam and Emily were decorating the individual tables in the dining area, humming Christmas carols while they worked, Pam heard a commotion.

"I've got to see Pam!" came to her ears. She hurried to the lobby.

Zeke and Josh stood barring Vic's way into the restaurant. She froze as Vic caught sight of her. "Why are you here?" she demanded.

Zeke glanced back at her. "We can remove him."

Vic shouted, "I'm leaving for Seattle, and I want to tell her goodbye!"

Taking a few steps forward, she hissed, "I have nothing to say to you. You lied to me and tried to hurt Tom. I don't care if I ever see you again!"

The Shafer brothers grabbed Vic by the arms and, while he struggled, tossed him out the lobby doors and then locked them. Pam dissolved into tears. "Why can't he leave me alone?" she wailed. Soon, she was enclosed by Addy and Emily and led to a chair, while Muriel brought a glass of water. Pam took a drink and dried her face with her handkerchief. "I'm sorry. I didn't mean to cause trouble."

Clamping both hands on her shoulders, Addy made Pam look at her. "It's not your fault." Addy glanced at her husband. "Vic seems to be obsessed with her."

Zeke paused a moment. "Well, at least he's leaving for the army. Otherwise, I think this could only be handled by the police."

Feeling bad, Pam stood and gave Muriel back the glass. "Thank you for the water. I'll get back to work."

Pam and Emily finished the table decorations, but the festive atmosphere was gone. Pam was polishing up the glassware behind the bar when Jenny came over, carrying two large mugs of coffee.

"Pam, take a break with me in the office."

Was Jenny going to tell her she was being let go? Pam tried to hide her shaking hands. "I'm sorry for what happened in the lobby. I'll understand if you want me to leave."

Jenny was speechless for a moment. "No, Pam.

You've been doing a wonderful job. I don't blame you for Vic's actions."

Feeling relieved, Pam took a sip of coffee. "Then what?"

"Remember you asked me what happened when Chase came by yesterday?" At Pam's nod, she continued, "He enlisted in the army and is supposed to leave January first for a six-month basic training. So the wedding in June is off. He'll be out of basic in July, but he won't know when or where he'll be deployed. Since I asked you to be one of the bridesmaids, I needed to tell you."

"What are you going to do?"

"I've been talking with him and my parents. We'll either get married at the courthouse before he leaves for basic or plan for a wedding in July." She sighed. "This war is making everything so hard. With food rationing going into effect, even at the restaurant, it's going to be difficult to know what we can serve from day to day."

"I remember Tom telling me that during the depression Mrs. Hutton said, 'You have to make do with what you've got.'"

Jenny's eyes lit up. "She did, didn't she? And she used to make the whole menu like it was today's special. She had a chalkboard, so she could change it every day, depending on what she could get." She jumped up and hugged Pam. "I knew there was a reason I wanted you to work here."

Waving her off, Pam retorted, "You would have figured it out for yourself, I know."

The two girls, all smiles, went back into the restaurant.

Chapter 5

Dear Tom,

I received a letter from Jen yesterday. Everyone's fine, but she and Chase have to postpone their wedding until July, because he doesn't get out of basic until then. So far, the army has told him he would have two weeks at home before he's deployed, but you and I know how the military goes, right? Anyway, he and Jen are planning to have a small wedding then. She said they will both understand if we can't make it.

Joe is in the installation here with me, and he says hello. I can't tell you where I am, but let's just say I believe we'll be fighting the Japs soon.

I heard from Pam, as well, and she told me not to tell you this, but just before Christmas our fathers had to toss Vic out of the theater. Seems he wanted to tell her goodbye before he went into the army. She didn't want to worry you, but I thought you should know. I'll apologize in my next letter to her.

Take care of yourself, Tom. I have to take my turn swabbing the floor. I'm on land assignment and they still want the decks mopped! Until then, I remain,

Hank

Tom ground his back teeth as he read the letter. *Well, at least Vic will be away from her for a while. I wish she would have told me this.* His thoughts were broken as Captain Allison entered the room. Tom jumped up to salute. "Yes, sir."

The captain returned the salute. "At ease, Shafer. I came in to give you a special assignment.

The mail plane came in, and the pilot has appendicitis. Since the surgery building here isn't finished, we need to ship him to the completed facilities at Fort Myers. Doc says there's no way the man should pilot in his condition. I know you've flown mail planes before, so you have the clearance to take both him and his plane there. You'll have to land at the naval airfield at Dutch Harbor, and they'll meet you with the ambulance. Stay overnight, and one of the mail planes will pick you and the nurse up tomorrow. Questions?"

"No, sir."

"Good. Be out at the airfield in ten minutes."

Tom saluted. "Yes, sir."

By the time he got to the airfield, the airplane was warming up and the invalid pilot was on a stretcher, a nurse beside him, on the deck. The pilot saluted Tom from where he lay. "Thanks for doing this. I'm Lieutenant Adams, from Elmendorf."

Tom smiled as he slid into the pilot's seat. "I'm Lieutenant Shafer, and I'll be your captain. I see Lieutenant Casey is your stewardess, the best-looking nurse on our base."

The dark-haired beauty gave him an intense gaze. "I'm here at your service."

Tom grinned and took off into the clear, cold sky. "We should have a smooth flight. It won't be more than twenty minutes."

Adams moaned when they went through some turbulence, but Tom maneuvered the plane out of it, and soon the airstrip at Dutch Harbor appeared in front of him. Tom eased the plane down as smoothly as he could and taxied to the waiting ambulance. Once Adams had been helped into the back of the vehicle, the nurse went in, as well.

Casey looked back at Tom. "Are you coming, too?"

He shook his head. "I'll help them with the

mail."

Shrugging, she gave a wave. "I'll see you later."

He waved back, and as the ambulance left the mail truck for the army and navy bases pulled up to the plane. Exiting from the vehicle, a big burly seaman shouted in Tom's direction. "Ahoy, Tom!"

He recognized his pal Joe Nikolaevich, Ivan and Kata's son. "Joe! I'll be damned! This is where you are?" Tom, Hank and Joe had been inseparable most of their lives, but keeping track of each other under the strict wartime regulations was impossible.

Joe grinned. "What's an army rat like you doing at Dutch Harbor?"

Tom told him of his mission.

"Come on and you can eat with Hank and me at the mess."

Just then, an army major drove up in a jeep. "Lieutenant Shafer? You're to come with me to Fort Myers. I'll show you your quarters for the night."

Tom saluted. "Sir, I was going to mess with my friend here."

"Sorry, Lieutenant. We need to know where you are and bring you back tomorrow so you can hitch a ride on the mail plane back to Umnak."

Tom sighed. "Yes, sir. Joe, tell Hank I'll write to him."

Slapping him on the shoulder, Joe sent Tom on his way. "Take care of yourself."

Reluctantly, Tom climbed into the back of the jeep. The major turned a stern eye on him. "I'm Major Johnson. You'll be bunking in the guest building. Lieutenant Casey will be with the other nurses. Both of you have to be ready at oh-eight hundred, and we'll transport you to the airfield."

Tom nodded. "Yes, sir."

At the fort, Tom stored his duffel bag in the guest quarters, inside one of the Quonsets with separate rooms, and headed to the mess. The wind was picking up sharply, and a few snowflakes were flying around like manic albino mosquitoes. He hunched into his jacket and sprinted the last few yards. Grabbing a tray and sliding into line, Tom heard someone come up behind him, and a female voice said, "Lieutenant Shafer, I was waiting for you. I hope you don't mind."

He looked into the sweet face of Lieutenant Casey. "No, I don't know anyone else here, either. My buddies are over at the airfield, too far away."

Going through the line, they picked up anything that seemed edible and then sat on one of the picnic-style tables set about the room.

"Lieutenant, how is Adams?"

Casey's green eyes sparkled as she smiled. "You can call me Mary now, if you want."

He chuckled. "Okay, if you'll call me Tom."

"Adams went through surgery and is right as rain, thanks to you."

He shook his head. "I was doing what I was ordered to do, but I would have anyway."

"Where are you from, Tom?"

"Me? I was born in Juneau. I used to fly the civilian mail plane before I joined the army. Where are you from?"

"New York. I'm a city girl. All this wilderness is hard to get used to."

They passed the mealtime talking and then continued their conversation at the O Club. Tom found he'd really missed a woman's companionship, and as the drinks went by, he flirted. Mary was a friendly girl and laughed easily. He might have been mistaken, but it seemed she flirted back, too.

As Tom walked her back to the nurses' quarters, she took his hand. "You know, I don't have to stay with the nurses—"

Tom took a sharp intake of the cold air. "Mary, I don't take advantage of girls. And I have a sweetheart at home."

Her eyes darkened. "I'm sorry. In more ways than you know." She kissed his cheek. "Sweet dreams, Lieutenant."

Watching her sashay through the door, he stood there a few moments. *If I did take her back to my quarters, would Pam ever know?* He chided himself at the thought. *She might not, but I would.* The guilt of what he was thinking sent him back to his room. *Am I the only one here who has never bedded a woman?* Pam was his one and only love through high school. He'd never dreamed of taking her before marriage, although they had petted heavily. *Would Pam benefit if I was more experienced?* He pondered this dilemma until he fell into a restless sleep.

The next day found the two lieutenants waiting on the tarmac for the mail plane. Mary had been quiet after a polite good morning in the mess. She had a quizzical look. "I hope you slept well last night."

Tom studied her face. "I did. I didn't turn you down because I didn't want to be with you. I just couldn't live with myself if I accepted your offer. I hope you understand."

She paused a moment. "I envy your sweetheart. She should know what a gem she has."

He smiled at the thought of Pam. "She's quite a gem herself."

"She must be." Mary gave him a quick kiss on the cheek as the mail plane taxied toward them. After Tom helped unload the sacks, they jumped in, and he hauled up the outgoing bags.

The surprised and grateful pilot thanked him for his help. "Usually officers don't bother with grunt work."

Tom grinned. "This was my profession before the army."

On their way to Umnak, the pilot turned to

Tom. "We've got sleet coming in a few hours. I may have to hold over at your base, depending on the weather."

"Sure, we're not swank with the amenities, but we've got room." Tom pointed out the window. "Any sign of the Japs yet?"

"No. They're still busy in the mid-Pacific, but I'll bet our turn is coming."

Tom looked silently over the turbulent sea. *You can train for war, but until you're in it, you don't even know what to prepare for.* But he knew the training he'd had would stand him in good stead. It already had, with Vic.

****

My dearest Pam,

Thank you for the birthday gift of the knitted scarf to go under my flight jacket. Anything to keep me warm is appreciated. My thoughts of you warm me, as well. The May sunshine is brightening things up here.

You asked me if the Japs have been sighted. The scout planes have located some of the subs, but they haven't come into the North Pacific that close. I believe that will change soon. They've been hitting our ships pretty hard south of us. Pray for me.

My mother tells me things are moving nicely for Jen's wedding. I'm sorry Hank and I can't be there, but we have a job to do. I know where he and Joe are. Maybe, one of these days, we'll run into each other.

I must cut this short, because we have emergency drills to do. Pam, I look at your picture every night before I sleep and dream of holding you. You're the only thing that keeps me sane here.

Always,

Tom

A month later, the early June sun belied the chilly breeze coming off the harbor. Pam straightened her back as she looked at the neat row of carrot seeds she'd just distributed in the restaurant garden behind the theater. Putting her hands on either side of the rich moist soil of the rows, she covered the seeds as gently as a mother covers her little one, loving the earthy smell that billowed up.

With food rationing on, the grassy area had become a tiny farm. Victory gardens, they were being called. Jen had decided the restaurant could be self-sufficient with its own fruit and vegetables, and all the waitresses could help with the gardening.

The wind played with the kerchief Pam had tied over her hair. She grabbed it before it got snatched away and looked at her watch. *I'd better get cleaned up. We'll be opening for dinner in a half hour.*

Hurrying through the kitchen door, Pam almost ran into Jen and Muriel. Jen grasped her hand. "Pam, we were going to have you come in."

Muriel put an arm around her. "We've just heard news on the radio that Dutch Harbor and Fort Myers were bombed by the Japanese these last two days."

Pam went numb. "Oh, no! Do you think that's where the boys are?"

The silence from both of them scared her. Following them to the office, she saw Zeke, Addy and Josh listening intently to the radio, and heard, "—smoke from the explosions could be seen from twenty miles away. The nearby air defenses were unable to stave off the attack."

Pam started trembling so badly she thought she would collapse, but Jen threw an arm around her shoulders and hugged her close. "We don't really know where they are stationed."

"Tom told me in one of his letters that he was in the North Pacific. He also said he knew where Hank and Joe are, and he hoped to see them. They must be near."

"I know. We got the same information from Hank." Pam stood next to Jen, listening to her heart pound. The two sets of parents sat in stunned silence.

Suddenly, Zeke stood. "Let's all get back to work. Take your minds off the war and put them into running this theater. The boys can take care of themselves." As he hustled everyone out of the office, Pam glanced at Addy's stricken face staring at Zeke and saw him take Addy into his arms. "Don't worry, love, I haven't taken leave of my senses. It will do us no good to sit and worry. We need to take care of things here."

As they left the office, Addy turned her tear-filled eyes to Pam, reaching out to squeeze Pam's hand. "Tom wouldn't want us to sit and worry, either. Come on."

Pam consigned the nagging fear to a far point in her brain and went to work. Zeke was right; doing something forced her to concentrate on the things at hand. But when she walked through the door at home, at the end of the workday, she looked at her parents and burst into tears.

Rushing to her side, her mother embraced her. "Honey, you heard the news?"

"Tom—I want to know how he is," Pam sobbed out.

Gripping her by the shoulders, her father shook her gently. "Until we hear anything one way or another, we shouldn't assume the worst."

Pam nodded sadly and, after a goodnight, headed to bed. Her prayers were strong and intense. "Dear Lord, keep Tom and the other boys safe. I know all won't come home, but give their families and loved ones the strength to go on. I may sound selfish, but I need Tom to live. Please. Amen." She stretched across her blanket while the slow tears soaked into it.

Chapter 6

Tom sucked in a shocked breath as he and Ken flew in formation with the squadron over Dutch Harbor. Embers and smoke rose from it and from Fort Myers. Japanese planes darted ahead of them. Umnak, because of the bad radio communications, hadn't gotten word of this attack until late. Stomach churning, Tom thought about Hank and Joe down there, and he prayed they were still alive.

Captain Allison's voice came over the radio. "Attack at will!" Tom and the others in his squadron peeled off from formation and went after the Jap planes. Tom's gut tightened, but his spine steeled as he let his training take over.

"Hey, Buck," Ken called over the radio with Tom's code name, "let's get that one!" He waved toward the closest one.

"Sure thing, Cowboy!" Tom sang out as they tailed the Zero.

They chased the Japanese west of Unalaska until the Zeros suddenly banked toward them. The one Tom and Ken were tailing came fast, guns flaring. Tom managed to dodge out of the way, but Ken's P-40 was hit a couple of times. "You all right?" Tom yelled into the radio.

"Doesn't look like he hit anything vital," Ken hollered back.

The Zero banked again, and Tom saw the perfect shot and took it. He managed to twist his plane out of range when the Zero's engine exploded.

"Yee-haa, pal, you got him! One down and four to go!" Ken's voice burst over the speaker.

Tom was on automatic pilot, doing what he was supposed to do, but something happened to him deep inside. He had killed another human being. In training, they had been told they were killing airplanes, but deep down Tom knew. A change came over him, different from anything he'd felt before. The horror of what he'd done was tempered by the realization that if he hadn't killed that Jap, he himself would have been killed. In that instant, he became a soldier.

The Zeros were hightailing it west when Captain Allison's voice boomed through the radio again. "We have clearance to land at Unalaska to refuel. When the scout planes let us know the Japs are out of the area, we can go home."

Tom taxied to the main hanger building at the Unalaska base. He left the airplane and had started toward the officer's mess when a familiar voice made him turn around. "Well, if it isn't the flyboy!"

Whirling around, Tom glared. "Vic, what the hell are you doing here?"

Setting down the garbage pail he was hefting, Vic took an aggressive stance. "I work here now, so you'd better watch your step."

A ruddy-faced sergeant hurried over and saluted Tom. "Is there any trouble here, Lieutenant?"

Returning the salute, Tom replied, "I'll take care of this, Sergeant."

"Yes, sir." The sergeant continued on his way.

Tom turned his attention to Vic. "Look, Private, things aren't the same way here as they were in Juneau. You're in the army now, and I outrank you. All I have to do is snap my fingers and you're going to live in the stockade. You hit me like you did in Juneau, you'll stay in the stockade the rest of the war. Do I make myself clear, Soldier?"

Vic glanced at the sergeant, who stood just out of earshot, then back at Tom. "Sir, yes, sir!" Vic's eyes flashed at Tom before he carried the trash away.

Ken met Tom at the door of the mess. "Who was that?"

"Juneau's town bully. He's after my girl, and I guess he thought if he got into uniform, she'd give a damn."

Ken snorted. "He looks like some of those big stupid bulls on my dad's ranch that butt into trees if they get in their way."

"That's probably why bullheaded describes Vic so well. Let's get something while the planes are being fueled."

They picked up coffee and a bite to eat, sitting at one of the tables. Captain Allison came over a few minutes later. "Get ready to head for Umnak in forty-five minutes. We'll debrief there."

"Yes, sir," they chorused.

Ken grinned at Tom. "Well done, for your first kill today. You'll make ace in a shake of a lamb's tail, if you keep that up. Four more will be a cinch."

Tom chewed slowly on his sandwich. "Thanks, Ken. In a way, I don't know quite what to feel. I've never killed anyone before."

Ken shrugged. "They're the enemy. Think of it as self-defense."

The atmosphere was getting foggy by the time the P-40s got back to Umnak. Ken's plane had been patched up nicely where the Zero had peppered it, but Tom and Ken found only six of the eight in their squadron made it back, shaking Tom to his core. Cory and Jake had been with the squadron since it was the Alaskan Defense Command. The feeling of mortality was strong. They took chairs in the debriefing room, then stood and saluted as Colonel Leland came in. "At ease, men. Sit."

One of his aides pulled down a map on the front wall before he handed the colonel a clipboard. "All set, sir."

"Thank you, Corporal." Picking up a pointer, Leland outlined on the map the area of yesterday's fighting as he read the report. "This was the first Japanese strike, but because of trouble in the radio communications we didn't get word of it until it was too late. Fort Myers was hit with an estimated fourteen bombs, destroying five buildings and an estimated twenty-five killed, the same casualty number. A second strike took no damage. A third strike destroyed a joint army-navy radio station. Two killed; a soldier and sailor. Questions?" He indicated someone in the back.

"Do we know what happened to the communication system?"

"Unknown at this time, probably atmospheric, but it worked this morning. This is unrelated, but it was reported that a Japanese Zero was forced to land at Akutan and was captured. So we can make a study of the aircraft. Question?"

Captain Allison stood. "Do we have the reports for today?"

"The strike took out four steel fuel tanks at Dutch Harbor with an approximate loss of twenty-two thousand barrels of oil. Casualties are still being counted, and the army lost five planes, including two from your squadron. Reports from the scout planes indicate the Japanese retreated west of Kiska. Be on alert for any news of another attack. Dismissed."

Tom went to his quarters with his heart in his throat. *I wish I knew if Hank and Joe were all right.* He resolved to write to Hank and hoped Hank would write back. He knew there would be civilian reports of the damage and fighting. *Pam, I made it through this one. Don't worry, and pray for me.*

****

Dear Pam,
I'm sure you've heard from my uncle and aunt

that Hank's still in the hospital at Dutch Harbor. I stopped by to see him when I had to go to Fort Myers for supplies. I still can't tell you where my base is. They've got me flying the transport plane occasionally, if there is no threat in the area. Hank got pretty banged up when the fuel tanks exploded in the bombing raid. Seems four ribs were broken, but he's on the mend and giving the staff grief.

Joe managed to escape injury and is helping to rebuild the base. He's as handy with construction as his old man. Tell Mr. and Mrs. Nikoleavich he's well and, like all of us, misses Juneau very much.

I know Jen's wedding is coming up soon. Chase may not have very much time at home before he's deployed. I hear they need troops in both Europe and the Pacific. I hope that's not spreading us out too thin, but I know we have to defeat both the Nazis and the Japs. Give my love and best wishes to Chase and Jen.

Save some of my love for yourself, my dear sweet girl. You have no idea how your letters give me the strength to go on. It's hard to see the empty beds after a battle, only to be filled up again with new soldiers. I should have a three-day pass one of these weeks, and I'll hitch a mail plane, if I can, to Juneau. I want to feel you in my arms again and kiss you thoroughly.

Thinking of you,

Tom

Pam picked the thorns off the rose stems before she inserted the fragrant blooms in the small centerpiece vases for each table in the restaurant for Jen and Chase's wedding reception. The radio was on at the end of the bar.

"—so far the Armed Forces have been able to prevent further invasion from the Japanese. They have confined the invaders to Attu and Kiska. Nothing has been heard from the radiomen at the stations there. It is feared they were taken prisoner."

Muriel waved at Pam. "Could you turn that off? I want the war gone today."

Pam turned the knob on the big dark wood console, shut the cabinet doors over it, and went back to work. Emily was up on a ladder, putting green crepe paper and white balloons around the wagon-wheel chandeliers.

Addy came in from the kitchen with the four-tiered layer cake, its green lattice design a background for the pink and red wild roses, made of sugar, cascading from the top and down one side. A ceramic bride and groom held court at the top, under an arch constructed of cardboard and green tissue paper. "Amelia really outdid herself this time," Addy remarked as she stood back and eyed it critically. "It's too bad Chase only has two weeks before he ships out to England."

Muriel shook her head. "Most of the others around here were deployed locally. I guess they're starting to need more in Europe."

Pam looked up. "It's sad Jenny and Chase won't have a long time before he has to leave."

Muriel nodded. "We've got them a couple of nights at the hotel downtown. Then they are going to room at his parents' home. Jenny will stay with us until Chase comes back." She sighed. "I hope this war is over soon."

Amelia came in from the kitchen. "I hope so, too. I used my whole allotment of sugar for that cake."

Muriel pursed her lips. "We can probably bring some from home, or use honey."

Emily came down from the ladder. "Pam, I'm going to go home and change for the reception. Would you like a ride home, too?"

Pam nodded. "Yes, thanks. I'll come back with my parents."

Waving, Addy moved them along. "See you at

two o'clock, then."

Zeke drove them, dropping Pam at her house where she greeted her parents before running upstairs to get ready. She'd meant to take only a quick bath, but even so she took time to relax and let the aromatic steam from the bubbles play around her nose.

Once dried off, Pam reached for the leg make-up, cursing the military for taking all the nylon in the country. Thank goodness for this alternative to stockings. Her legs turned a light tan color as she smoothed it on, carefully putting it on evenly to just above her knees. Then she took her eyebrow pencil and drew in a seam on the back of her legs while she sat at her vanity, carefully checking her work with a hand mirror.

Getting dressed, she pulled her petal-pink satin dance dress out of the closet. The soft folds of the material slid over her skin like a caress. After straightening the flutter sleeves and tying the sash in the back, she looked at herself in the full-length mirror, remembering how Tom loved that dress on her.

From her dresser she picked up the gold-framed picture of Tom in his uniform, a mischievous grin on his face. *I wish you were here with me. I hate going anywhere without you.* She ran a finger down Tom's cheek and gave the photo a kiss before setting it down, and then, seated at her vanity, she brushed her shoulder-length hair. Taking a comb, she parted it on the side in Veronica Lake style; the golden strands dipping over one eye. *No, that's going to annoy me.* Instead, she placed a hair clip to hold it out of her face. As she applied her makeup, she wondered who she was trying to impress. She didn't have a date for the reception; Tom wouldn't be there. *I guess I just like dressing up once in a while.*

"Come on, princess, we're ready to go!" her

father called from downstairs.

Quickly slipping on her pumps and grabbing her purse, Pam hurried down. The family piled into the Packard and headed to the Golden North. Only their parents went to the courthouse with Jen and Chase for the wedding itself, but on their return they formed a reception line in the lobby of the theater where they greeted all their guests.

As the Wrights waited their turn in line, Pam noticed there were many men in uniform as guests. *Must be a lot of Chase's friends from basic. So many of the young men in Juneau are in the service now.*

Pam smiled as she greeted Muriel and Josh. Muriel hugged her, then greeted the rest of her family. Josh gave her a kiss on the hand. "You look beautiful tonight, Pam. It's a lucky thing—" He stopped talking when Muriel dug her elbow in his side.

Jenny was next and threw her arms around Pam. "Thank you for coming!" She wore a white tailored suit with a shoulder-length veil that set off her dark brown hair and light olive skin.

"You look radiant, Jen. Best wishes to you and Chase." She kissed Chase on the cheek. "I'll pray for you on your deployment, and to come home soon."

He grinned at her and squeezed her hand. "Thank you, Pam."

She greeted Chase's parents, whom she barely knew, and went on into the restaurant with her family behind her. Scanning the crowd, she spotted Addy talking with a tall soldier in dress uniform, his back to the door. When he turned in her direction, Pam dropped her purse to the floor. "Tom!" she screamed. Everything stopped, and the only person she could see in the room was making his way to her.

"Oh, my dear sweet girl!" he said as he pressed his lips on hers and enveloped her in his arms.

Pam ran her hands over his face and down his shoulders as if she couldn't believe he was really there. "It's been almost a year," she said as she pulled back to look at him. "How are you here?"

Tom laughed. "I had a three-day pass coming, so I took it in Juneau. I have to go back to base tomorrow."

"I thought you had three days."

"I traveled here yesterday and arrived late, so the end of my time is when I travel back tomorrow. That's why I don't usually come this way on a three-day pass."

Suddenly, Pam was embarrassed because everyone was watching them. "I'm sorry, I didn't mean to make a spectacle of myself."

Addy hugged her. "We've been planning this surprise since yesterday."

Returning Pam's purse to her, Pam's mother had an amused smile. "Addy, your brother-in-law almost gave it away, but I don't think Pam caught it."

Addy shook her head and laughed. "Josh was never very good at secrets."

Soon, the wedding party joined everyone in the restaurant, where the spaghetti dinner was enjoyed by all. They had to save what meat they had for the restaurant meals. The entrée was served with hot garlic bread and salad fresh from the restaurant's garden. After the cake was cut, the record player kept them dancing into the evening.

Pam and Tom never left each other's side except for one dance Tom had with Jenny. At the end of one of the dance pieces, Tom took Pam's arm and led her to the stairs to the second floor where they sat on the steps halfway up. "Pam, I have to talk to you."

A shudder of anticipation went through her. *Is he going to ask me to marry him?* "What is it?"

"Now that I've been in combat, I'm concerned

that something might happen to me." He squeezed her hand. "The only reason I haven't asked you to marry me is that I don't want to make you a young widow. I want to make sure I come out of this alive before I make that commitment to you."

Tears blurred her eyes. "I've never seen you like this."

"I'm telling you this, just in case you were wondering why I hadn't brought up the subject of marriage. As soon as this war is ended, I want you to be with me always, as you are here." He patted his shirt pocket. "I guess you could call this—an unofficial engagement? I don't have a ring yet, to seal it."

Pam swallowed hard and took both his hands in hers, to press them to her lips.

"Sweetheart, war is not a glorious thing. It's ugly. Death comes very easily out there. I remember my mother telling me about her grandfather, who went into the Civil War when he was nineteen, and how he never talked about it. I understand why." He moved his hands from hers and pulled out metal tags that were on a chain around his neck. "We have to wear these to identify us, if anything happens—"

Her hand closed around the tags, still warm from his body. "Tom, I wish we didn't have to go through this war, but I understand what you're saying. There's no one I would ever consider marrying other than you. I want to be your strength, your love. I will wait for you."

Pulling the clip from her hair, he ran his fingers through the strands, then gripped the back of her head and drew her toward him. They kissed deeply, her eyes overflowing and her senses recognizing only his scent, his touch, storing this in her memory to take out when she needed to remember. She spiraled down the eddy of desire for him, letting her hands run over every inch of him, as his did to her, wanting to know more.

Finding his breath, Tom gazed deep into her eyes. "Oh, my love, how I want you. I need nothing more than to make love to you, but we can't take that chance on your reputation."

Pam shook her head. "I'd even give that up to have you."

"No, I couldn't do that to you. You know how narrow-minded the people are here."

She clung to him for a few moments and knew he was wise in what he said. "Let's freshen up and go back to the party." She rose and pulled him up to join her.

Soon, Jenny and Chase were ready to depart for the honeymoon suite at the top hotel in town. The limo was waiting outside the theater, and everyone went out to see them off. Jenny held Tom in a hug for a few seconds longer. "I know you won't be here when I get back. Take care of yourself, cousin."

"I will." Tom turned to Chase. "Watch out for yourself in Europe."

Chase shook his hand. "Give the Japs trouble, and I'll take a whack at the Nazis."

Holding each other, Pam and Tom watched the limo drive out of sight. Her heart ached, she so wanted to have what Jen and Chase had.

The remaining guests returned to the dining room and danced for a few more songs, but before long the party broke up. Pam's family was ready to go, and her father tapped her on the shoulder.

"Pam, come on." He turned toward the door.

There was a huge lump in her throat. She didn't want to let go of Tom. He walked her to the entrance, where he kissed her thoroughly, and she didn't care who saw. He pulled back. "Eight o'clock at the airfield."

"Wild horses won't keep me away." She ran a hand down his cheek, and he gently took her fingers and put them to his lips.

The next morning found them locked in an embrace at the airfield, while the mail plane waited. Pam wanted to remember everything about Tom and keep him in her mind. She wished she could stop time right there, and he wouldn't have to go.

He'd already said his goodbyes to his family and, as he turned, she made an attempt to keep grasping his hand. He smiled. "I love you, you know."

Pam mouthed, "I love you, too," for no sound came from her throat.

Tom blew her a kiss as he disappeared inside the plane. Pam stood with the wind ruffling her hair, watching the plane carrying her beloved take off. She turned with a heavy heart and made her way to the little group who waited for her.

Chapter 7

Tom watched through the window as Dutch Harbor came into view, and the pilot turned to him. "I have a layover for a couple of hours here before I continue to Umnak."

Checking his watch, Tom nodded. "That's all right. I still have plenty of time to get to the base. I have a cousin and a friend here I want to see. I'll be at the tarmac when you're ready."

Tom got directions to the hospital building and found Hank in one of the wards, with Joe seated in a chair by the bed. Hank's ribs were taped and he was propped up with the pillow, but he had that old sparkle in his eyes. "Tom! What are you doing here?"

"I managed to get a three-day pass, so I went to Jen and Chase's wedding. The mail plane I hitched on has a two-hour layover here before it goes back."

Standing, Joe shook his hand. "Tom, it's good to see you."

Hank pointed to the foot of the bed. "Sit there and tell me how everything is going at home."

Tom related all the news he could think of about the families and the wedding. "How are you doing?"

Patting the bandages, he said, "They've got it so tight, I look like Frankenstein when I get up. It still hurts some, but it's manageable."

Just then, an attractive nurse balancing a lunch tray came over. "Well, Mr. Shafer, it looks like you've got company. I know Mr. Nikoleavich, but who is the army man?"

"That's my cousin, Tom Shafer. Tom, meet Patsy O' Day."

Tom shook her hand, taking in the auburn hair tucked neatly under her nurse's cap and a pair of beautiful emerald eyes sizing him up. "Pleased to meet you, Miss O' Day."

"And how did you know I'm a Miss?"

Tom pointed to her ringless finger.

"Oh, you Shafer boys are smarties, aren't you?" She set Hank's tray on his nightstand and then blushed as Hank gently grasped her hand.

"Thank you, Patsy." The young nurse went back to the other trays without another word.

Tom smiled after her. "Who's working on whom?"

Hank glowed. "She's something, isn't she?"

"Are you going home after you get out of here?"

"No, they don't think this is serious enough to give me a discharge, so the navy still has me."

Tom turned to Joe. "I imagine the rebuilding has kept you busy."

A troubled look came into Joe's eyes. "Yes, but I've had some assignments, too." He glanced at Hank. "I had to help with some of the evacuations of the islanders last month. I tell you, Tom, that's probably the hardest thing I ever had to do. The Aleuts were treated so badly by the government. I told my folks about it."

Tom shook his head. "They didn't say anything about it to me."

"I was a hand on one of the patrol crafts that went to St. Paul to notify the community that they were to be evacuated. Then we helped the people onto the USAT Delarof. The next day, we anchored off of St. George Island for the whites who wished to leave."

Tom pressed his lips together. "Just the whites?"

"At first. Then, later, word came down that the whole community would need to leave." Joe was silent for a moment. "Tom, those poor people had only one hour to pack a suitcase and grab some blankets before they were loaded on the ship. And then Dan Benson, the caretaker, was ordered to destroy the village with gasoline and dynamite." Sadness warred with anger on his face. "You should have seen those families watching all their possessions go up in smoke, everything except for what they carried with them."

"Why was the village destroyed?"

"The word was, if the Japs invaded the area, there should be no supplies for them. Anything they could use to their advantage against us had to be damaged beyond repair. No food left for their troops, either."

"Where were the people taken?"

Joe snorted. "To Killisnoo. The abandoned cannery building."

Tom was astonished. "But that has no heat or electricity."

Joe nodded and his fist hit his knee. "Right. They didn't get any help at first, either. My mother wrote to me that a nurse went over there *one* day and never went back. No one in Juneau has lifted a finger to help them. My uncle and aunt in Angoon went with a number of other Tlingits to give them fish and other food, to keep them from starving." He looked Tom in the eye. "What the hell are we doing?"

Tom glanced at Hank, who shrugged. Tom pursed his lips. "I know we're not supposed to question our superiors, but that sounds terrible, to me."

Joe shook his head. "I guess there isn't much grunts like us can do about it." He rose. "I've got to get back to work. It's good seeing you again, Tom." The boys shook hands, and Joe departed.

Settling into the chair Joe had vacated, Tom glanced at Hank. "That seems like an awful thing to do to our people."

Hank sighed. "Most people I know don't consider Aleuts 'our people.' I think it hit Joe hard because of his mother's family. They might have gotten citizenship, but not respect."

Changing the subject, Tom leaned toward Hank. "Did they give you any idea when you're going to be released?"

"Looks like another week or so. How's Pam?"

Tom grinned. "Beautiful. When I get out of this hellhole, I'm going to marry her as soon as I can." He looked down. "I want to make sure I get out of this alive." He was silent for a moment.

Hank regarded him with a frown. "Something is bothering you. What?"

"Female personnel. Hank, I was tempted to sleep with a particular young lady and found I had a hard time saying no."

"But you did say no. Hell, I've been tempted by many a dame. That's not love, it's lust. We've got to resist it. You love Pam, right?" At Tom's nod, Hank continued, "Do you love this other young lady?"

"I don't feel the same way with her, but there's an attraction."

"Just think about who you want to spend your life with."

Tom spent the rest of his time telling Hank more about the folks back home.

****

Dear Pam,

We have been busy bombing the Japs and we've been hitting them pretty hard. Here's hoping we can keep them at bay. The October skies are always drizzly, and I think they hide us well enough that the Japs haven't been able to detect us.

I know Hank and Patsy were able to take leave at the same time and visit the folks back home. I thought when I first met her there was an attraction between those two. They couldn't start seeing each other until Hank got out of the hospital, but they sure made up for lost time. What did you think of Patsy?

Joe has been down about the way the Aleuts have been treated at the various places they were evacuated to. It seems nobody wants them in their backyard. I swear the Japs in the American camps are being treated better.

Well, enough of the bad thoughts. Pam, thoughts of you pull me out of the dumps many times. You are the shining light at the end of this horror, and I can't wait to get home to you.

All my love and kisses,

Tom

Pam helped Muriel and Addy put up the heavy black curtains across the inside of the theater lobby doors. The men were switching off the outside lighted signs in accord with the blackout rules the government had sent them. It seemed all of the west coast cities were under civil defense warnings.

Jenny slipped between the drapes and hugged her mother. "I got the test back from the doctor. I'm going to have Chase's child."

Muriel was elated. "That's wonderful news! We've got to send a telegram to England at once."

Addy put her hands on her hips and her lips edged up. "Well, my dear, you're a grandmother before I am."

Muriel hugged both Jenny and Addy, laughing. "You know something? I don't care. It's been so long since we've had little ones around here."

"The doctor said it should be here toward the end of April."

Pam congratulated her with a hug.

A few minutes later, the men came down from the roof. Zeke wiped his hands on his work overalls. "We left all the electric cables in the rooms upstairs."

As Josh came down, Muriel grinned. "Well, here is Grandpa Josh!"

Josh stopped for a moment, then Pam saw dawn shine on his face. He hugged Jenny and spun her around. "You're expecting?" She nodded. "That's terrific!"

An hour later, Pam was helping Jenny set the bar up for the evening and noticed Jen was quiet and sullen. Pam put her hand on Jen's arm. "Is something wrong?"

Jen looked up and sighed. "I was thinking what Chase said about me running the restaurant in my condition."

"Oh, yes, he wanted you to quit when you started a family." She bit her lip. "Jen, it really would make sense for you to keep working until Chase comes home. You don't have a home of your own, and you have family to look after you here."

"We chose a poor time to start a family."

"That isn't always our choice." The two girls leaned on each other.

Jenny smiled. "If Tom doesn't marry you, I'll never forgive him."

Zeke drove Pam home after work. As she waved goodbye to him, she heard movement in the hedges lining the yard on either side. An eerie chill went through her as she stopped and looked around. *It feels like someone's watching me.* She shook it off. *That's silly. It's probably an animal rooting around for winter food.* She moved quickly toward the house and, as she opened the door, she heard a rustling again that made her jump and close the door with a bang.

Her father came into the hallway. "What's the matter?"

Trying to get her feelings in order, Pam was silent for a few moments. "I heard a rustling outside as I came up the walk. It seemed to come from the hedges."

He shook his head. "It was probably some

animal gathering food for the winter."

She hesitated. "I felt like I was being watched."

He went outside and looked among the hedges and around the porch. Sighing, he came in. "Pam, you're letting your imagination run away with you."

She glanced down at the tips of her shoes. "I'm sorry, Dad. I guess I'm jumpy tonight." Pam leaned in the living room door to tell her mother goodnight and chastised herself as she went to her room upstairs. *What's the matter with me? I guess I'm letting the October ghosts in early.* She gazed out the window, only to see a shadowy figure disappear around the corner from their driveway to the sidewalk. She drew back in alarm. *I know I saw that. Vic? Why do I think it's him? But it can't be him. He's not even in town.* Pam slept fitfully that night.

Her mother studied Pam with concern when she sat down to breakfast the next morning. "Honey, you look beat. What's the matter?"

Pam concentrated on buttering her toast. "I guess I didn't sleep very well last night."

Her father glanced at her. "Does it have anything to do with what happened?"

Pam pressed her lips together. "When I got upstairs, I saw someone slip around from our driveway to the sidewalk."

"Are you sure?"

"Yes. I wasn't mistaken."

Her parents regarded each other, and her mother chewed on her lip. "Maybe we should let the authorities know about this."

Her father tapped the stem of his pipe on his mouth. "I'll talk to Sheriff Lindsey before I go to the airfield." Turning to Pam, he said, "Do you have any idea who it is?"

"No, I couldn't see a face. If I didn't know that Vic was away in the army, I might have thought it was him."

That afternoon, Pam chipped ice from a block at the bar. Coming in before she went to the dressing rooms to get ready for the play, Emily stood by her. "Hi, Pam. It looks like a great crowd tonight." Emily took one of the ice chips and sucked on it thoughtfully. "By the way, did you hear Vic is in town on leave?"

A shock went through Pam's body, and she dropped the ice pick. "Vic is in town?"

"Pam, you're pale as a sheet. What's wrong?"

Pam told her of the rustling hedges and what she'd seen last night.

"Do you think Vic was sneaking around your house?"

"I don't know, Em, but somehow I suspect him."

Muriel appeared from the office door. "Pam, Sheriff Lindsey is here to see you." She waved her hand behind her. "You can use the office."

Going in and closing the door, Pam greeted him. The sheriff sat on one of the wooden chairs in front of the desk, and she seated herself in one of the others, facing him. "You wanted to see me?"

He nodded. "Miss Wright, your father spoke to me this morning about an incident that happened last night at your home."

"Yes, I heard a rustling in the hedges, and when I looked out my bedroom window, I noticed someone leaving our driveway, going to the sidewalk."

"Do you have any idea who it was?"

"No, I didn't see his face."

"Do you have a hunch who it could be?"

Wrestling whether she should accuse Vic or not, Pam was silent for a moment. "I heard Vic Houston was back in town on leave."

"You think it was Vic at your house last night?"

"I don't know who else it could be."

The sheriff made a few notes on a paper pad, then flipped it shut. "You know about the incident last year, when Vic and a couple of his friends tried to beat up Tom Shafer."

At her nod, he continued, "I believe Mr. Houston has a fixation on you. I've heard of men like that trying to kidnap the girl, or trying to hurt her in some way. Or worse. I could pick him up on suspicion of trespassing, but until he does anything, I can't charge him."

"What should I do?"

"There's safety in numbers. As long as he's in town, don't go anywhere by yourself. I would warn your family and friends to be on the watch for him, too."

Pam, lost in thought, managed to reply, "Thank you for your advice. I guess he won't be here long, anyway."

"I know this is frustrating for you. I wish I could do more."

Pam watched him leave before she went back to work. For the next few days, someone was always with her, and her father bought a guard dog for their home. Her brother promptly named the German shepherd Rin-Tin-Tin.

Chapter 8

My dear son,

I'm sure someone has told you that Jen is expecting in April. She has been busy getting the restaurant business set up properly for her mother to take over for a week or so, when she delivers the baby. (Even though it's still six months away. You know how Jen is.) Chase is happy about it. He even agreed that Jen could still work at the restaurant until he gets back. There should be enough of us to help with the little one here.

Em has taken over the role of Yukon Lil since she graduated from high school. I guess this old horse should be put out to pasture. Dave has taken the male lead, and your dad and I are in the chorus. Dave and Em are becoming an item.

I know Pam wouldn't want me to mention this, but she had trouble with Vic. He was on leave and spying on her. The sheriff gave her some advice and her father bought a German Shepherd to guard their house. Don't worry, we will all take care of her here.

Stay safe. You're my firstborn, and I love you and pray for you every day.

Your Mother

The hanger at Fort Myers boomed with sounds of the band. The general had thought a dance would be a morale builder right before Christmas. Tom and Ken approached the entrance, battling the December winds that threatened to carry them off without their planes.

Tom turned to Ken and shouted to him over the music. "It's too bad we couldn't combine parties with the navy."

"I know you have a friend and a cousin in the navy, but the head honchos figure there would be too many fights in the building."

The boys strode to the bar and brought a couple of beers to a table ahead of the crowd. When the band took a break, everyone scrambled either to a seat or to the bartender. Balloons and crepe streamers floated on the waves of body heat.

In a couple of hours, Tom sat nursing one beer after another while Ken took the floor with some of the female personnel. Tom felt too vulnerable to do the same. Ken slapped Tom on the back after one of his forays. "You can't sit here all night! Grab one of the dames and hoof it to the music." He took his bottle and swung into his chair.

Tom took a peek at him. "I'm not that good of a dancer."

"Oh, meadow muffins! Hey, hello—"

The two other chairs at the table were pulled out, and two girlish figures sat themselves down. Tom turned his beer-soaked brain to the new members of the circle. The familiar flash of Mary Casey's green eyes arrested him.

"Well, if it isn't Lieutenant Tom! How ya doin', handsome? My friend is Bobbie Sue Sommers from Austin, Texas."

The sunny-haired Bobbie Sue was already on Ken's radar, and he stuck out his hand. "Pleased to meet you. Let's dance, beautiful." Pulling her up, he had her out on the floor in no time.

Swaying a bit, Tom rose from his chair. "If you'll excuse me for a minute—" He made his way to the men's room, secretly hoping she would go someplace else while he was in there. On his trip back to the table, he could see her at the table yet, sipping her drink. *Damn, she's still there.*

"Aren't you interested in dancing?" she mused as

he sat again.

"You're dangerous, Mary."

A smile played on her lips. "Really? That's good to know."

"You're a lovely young lady, and you're here. That makes you a woman to avoid."

"Hmm, there's some attraction here." She took hold of his tie and drew him to her.

Tom stood again. "Do you want to dance?"

She studied him for a moment. "Love to." The band launched into "Always" and Mary pressed herself tightly into Tom's arms, stepping to a slow waltz. "I thought I heard you tell your friend you weren't a good dancer."

He attempted to whirl her around and managed to step on both her feet. "I'm sorry. I've had too many beers for this." At the end of the number, she ran her hands up his chest and kissed him. Tom felt her probing tongue, and his groin tightened as she rubbed up against him. "Mary, I—"

She put her fingers on his lips. "Shh, come with me." Grabbing his arm, she used the confusion of people exiting the dance floor to lead him into a small hall off to the side, trying a couple of doors until she found one that was unlocked. A storage room.

Following her in and shutting the door, Tom pinned Mary against it, asking, "What do you want?"

"You." She unbuttoned her uniform shirt and pulled it out of her skirt, while Tom planted kisses down her neck to her shoulder. Between the beer and the lust, all he could see was a willing female, and his basic instincts took over. Undoing his tie and shirt, she ran her tongue up the underside of his chin.

Tom moaned and she unhooked her brassiere to allow him access to her gorgeous breasts, the nipples hardening under his hands, and she purred deep in her throat.

As she pulled his shirt from him, the picture of Pam fell out of the pocket and, face up on the floor, stared at him accusingly. Breath rasping, Tom stopped, his eyes moving from the picture to Mary, his knuckles whitening as he clasped his fists. "I can't do this to her!" he said hoarsely.

She grabbed him, her breath coming through her deliciously moist lips. "Please?"

"I'm sorry, Mary. I said you were dangerous." He put his shirt and tie back on. "You're a hell of a woman, Mary Casey, but I can't be your man. I love this woman"—he shook the small photo at her—"too much to mess it up." He replaced Pam's picture and, as Mary was buttoning up her shirt, opened the door to a sound in the hall, but when he checked, nothing was there.

Mary was put together, and they both went back to the dance. "You're really something, Tom Shafer," she said.

He grinned at her. "I know."

She planted herself in front of him. "I want to let you know, I won't stop trying." There was a determined glint in her eyes. Before he could stop her, she gave him a thorough kiss, then sashayed into the crowd.

Tom shook his head to clear it and started to the table he shared with Ken, who was forehead to forehead with Bobbie Sue, so Tom decided to call it a night. Bundled up, he sprinted to his quarters.

Still feeling the effect of the beers, he collapsed onto his bed. *I didn't realize I'd have several battles to fight.* But his main concern was how far he would have gone if Pam's picture hadn't appeared. That's what scared him.

****

Pam,
You should know that Tom has been seen with a

nurse named Mary Casey. At a dance, he disappeared into a storeroom with her.

A friend

Pam looked at the note as if it had been sent from the moon. *Who would write this, I wonder? Someone who wants to break us up? Could it be Vic?*

Coming to her across the living room, her mother put her hand on Pam's arm. "What's wrong, sweetheart? You seem so bewildered."

Pam showed her the letter. "Why would someone send me this?"

Her mother quickly read the note. "Honey, this isn't even signed. Do you know who it's from?" At a shake of Pam's head, her mother continued, "This person must have some grudge against Tom and wants to cause trouble. Tom seems to love you. I would wait until you can talk to him face to face."

Pam swallowed hard. "Could this be true?"

"Pamela! Don't jump to conclusions. Believe in Tom until you have proof of this. Has he ever lied to you?"

"No."

"Then give him the benefit of the doubt."

The note weighed on her mind that afternoon at the restaurant. Pam stayed to herself when she wasn't waiting on tables, and caught Jen watching her with a concerned expression. She cornered Pam by the kitchen door. "Pam, something's bothering you. What is it?"

"It's nothing. I'm tired, that's all."

"That's not a tired look, and you aren't usually this quiet."

Pam sighed and told Jen about the note.

"I know my cousin as well as I know myself. Tom would never do that to you behind your back. Where was it sent from?"

Pam thought for a moment. "I'm pretty sure it had an APO address. It was signed, 'A friend.'"

"Well, I'll tell you, that was no friend of yours. I agree with your mother; wait until you can talk to Tom."

Pam smiled and hugged Jen, but the nagging little doubt still gnawed at her. The Shafers were setting up the Christmas tree in the restaurant as the dinner guests thinned out. A couple of army officers came in as she took a tray of dishes to the kitchen for the washer, but she had already arranged for a short break and stepped outside for a smoke. Slipping through the door on her way back to work, she heard a scream and a cry. The movie was going on in the theater, but the sound didn't come from there. It seemed to come from the office.

None of the Shafers were about, but then the office door opened and the two army officers she had seen earlier came out with Zeke, who looked shaken. Pam's heart dropped to the floor, and she gripped the back of the nearest chair.

Oh, God, did something happen to Tom? She wavered between running into the office to find out and waiting to see if someone would tell her.

Glancing at Pam, Zeke escorted the officers out the lobby doors before he made his way over to her. She gripped his arm. "What—who?"

He put his hand over hers. "Not Tom." He took a second to compose himself. "They were here to tell Jenny that Chase was killed in Europe."

Pam's throat closed and tears misted her eyes. "Oh, no! Poor Jenny." She started trembling and pulled out the chair to sit down. "How?"

Zeke sat next to her. "They said it was in an assault on Naples, a few days ago. They're sending his effects back to her."

"If there is anything I can do, let Jenny know she can count on me."

"I'll tell her. Are you going to be all right?"

Pam nodded. Zeke patted her shoulder as he

rose and headed to the office.

****

A week later, the day before Christmas, a silent snow gently fell around the church where Pam and her family gathered with the Shafers and the Marshalls, and other friends and relatives, for the service in memory of Chase.

All that Jenny had of her husband came in a shipping box. His dog tags and mementos were all there. Jenny had been inconsolable when she found the telegram in his wallet about their baby. *He must have been so happy*, Pam thought. *But now...*

The memorial service was impressive in its military traditions. Pam and her family sat behind the Shafers and the Marshalls in their church, watching the local soldiers stand at attention as the eulogies from the minister and family members went on. Pam glanced at Jenny, who sat between her mother and her mother-in-law, clasping their hands as if for strength. Pam's heart was breaking for Jen and her baby. Far back in her mind, where she had sent it, was the awareness that this could happen to Tom.

As they left the church, the snow had ended and the heavens were clear in the crisp air. One of the young soldiers was playing "Taps" hauntingly beneath the northern lights that waved like a tribute in the dark sky. All the others, in turn, offered condolences to Jenny and the Marshalls.

The group of people silently turned, heading back to their cars, their feet making swishing noises in the white December snow. Pam looked up at the stars. *Please, God, bring us peace on earth this next year.*

She found it hard to go back to the gaily decorated restaurant and work, but she knew the Shafers needed everyone to pitch in while their family tried to heal from this tragedy. This, certainly, put the letter about Tom into perspective. *Worrying about something like that, when Jen has lost her husband...* She helped shut down the restaurant that evening, closing it until the day after Christmas.

In the lobby, she peered at a figure in black in the dim light, sucking in her breath in fear it might be Vic as the person turned toward her. "Jenny?"

Jenny hesitated a moment. "Pam, I had to come back here tonight. I needed to find something normal."

"Is there anything I can do?"

Jenny embraced her. "I don't know how I'm going to get through this. I never expected Chase—well, I mean, this was never in our plans." Pam silently waited for her to go on. "Thank you for being there."

Muriel came in. "Jenny, ready to go home?"

Jenny stood back and nodded.

As they were going out the door, Muriel turned. "Do you need a ride?"

Gesturing toward the street, Pam said, "My dad's waiting for me." Drawing her coat around her, Pam put her arms around both of them. "I know this isn't a happy time, but may the Christmas Peace be with all of you."

Muriel kissed Pam's cheek. "Thank you. To you as well."

On their way home, Pam's dad drove by the Marshalls' house. The blue star in the window was now gold.

Chapter 9

Dear Tom,

Jenny seems to be doing all right, although the loss of Chase and the worry about what to do when the baby comes consumes her. Your Aunt Muriel has done much to help her through this. She told me she was a widow when Jenny was born. I guess the only one who truly understands is one who has been there.

I know you said you have a leave coming up in February. I need to talk to you, and it's not something I want to write about, so I'll wait until you're home.

All my love,

Pam

Tom looked around uneasily as he climbed out of the transport plane onto the airfield at Juneau. The first people he saw were his family, and then his father nudged him and he noticed Pam standing by the mail office with her father. Tom had been concerned that the last few letters from her hadn't been as warm, and he didn't know what was different. *Was it because of Chase's death? Have I said something to upset her somehow?*

Pam's breath floated in the cold morning air as she took hesitant steps toward him. "Welcome home, Tom." She embraced him, but with some stiffness in her.

"Something's bothering you, sweetheart. What is it?"

She turned to her father. "Dad, can Tom and I talk in your office for a moment?"

He nodded. "I have to help with the mail, so go ahead."

She took Tom's hand and drew him into the building. After closing the door, she faced him with a determined look. "Who is Mary Casey?"

Tom felt faint and wavered a moment.

Pam teared up. "So you do know a Mary Casey." She sat hard on one of the chairs, as if stricken.

"How do you know about Mary?" As soon as he asked that question, he wanted to call it back. Pam frowned and handed him a note, and he knew he must be pale, reading the condemning paper. Folding it up, he said, "You know I never lied to you, and I won't start now." He pulled air into his lungs as she stared at him. "Yes, this is true."

Slumping in the seat, she buried her face. "Oh, Tom—"

He put his hands on her shoulders. "But nothing happened. I don't remember how many beers I had at that dance, but I was tempted. When we got into the storeroom, your picture fell out of my pocket, and I couldn't do anything but pick it up and get out of there. I love you, Pam." He ran his fingers down her arms, then raised her palms to his lips.

Gently withdrawing her hands, she looked hurt. "And what would have happened if my picture hadn't fallen out?"

He gazed at her and said quietly, "I know I'm only offering up excuses for myself. There's no reason why I should have put myself in that situation." He raised her chin. "Look at me. I'm truly sorry for what I did. I don't love Mary, all I felt for her was lust. I can only hope I would have stopped myself in any case."

She buried her face, again, and sat motionless for a few moments.

Oh, God, have I lost her? Will she be able to forgive me? "Pam, I'm so sorry to put you through this. Please accept my apology." Putting her hands down, she regarded him sadly. "I love you too much

91

to do that to you." He reached for her.

Pam stood and hugged him. "At least you're honest with me. I do forgive you." With their kiss Tom could feel her body relaxing in his embrace. *I don't want to lose this. God, give me strength to resist the "Marys" of this world.*

He looked at the note again. "Do you have any idea who sent this?" So he *had* heard something just before he opened the storage room door that night.

She shook her head. "It wasn't signed, and there wasn't any name on the envelope."

When Tom strode out of the office with Pam on his arm, his eyes locked with his father's, which held a question. At Tom's nod, his dad smiled.

Putting her arm around Tom, his mother confided, "Emily and Dave are going to take on the season opener of *Gold Rush* tonight. You two will be in the front row."

Tom gave her an amazed glance. "I can't believe you're stepping back, Mom."

She sighed. "Sometimes you have to admit when your children are right. Em is very good, and I am getting gray."

Tom smirked. "Couldn't Edna give you a color rinse? I hear older women do that all the time."

Glaring at him, his mother stopped, putting her hands on her hips. His father shook his finger at Tom. "Now you've done it."

Through her teeth, Mom hissed, "I'm not old! I'm just mature enough to know when to keep my thoughts to myself!" She huffed and stalked to the car. Pam suppressed a giggle as Tom grinned.

Tom's dad parked in back of the theater and everyone went in through the kitchen door. Amelia and Jenny were going over the evening's menu when Jenny looked up and spotted Tom. Her face had several emotions written on it from joy to sadness. Flying into Tom's arms, she burst into sobs, and he held her tight. "Jen, I'm so sorry about Chase. I wish I could have been here for you."

He gazed at her red, tear-streaked face as she said, "Please, Tom, come home safe after the war. If anything happens to you, Hank, or Joe, I don't know what I'll do."

Hearing the commotion, Muriel hurried into the room. Tom gave a sign for her to wait. "Jen, listen to me. I'd love to promise that, but I can't. We all chose to do this for our country. Be proud of Chase, because he died doing what he believed in. It must hurt now, but it will get better. You have to be strong for your little one."

Putting her arm around her daughter, Muriel guided her out the door. "Thank you, Tom. Jenny will be better with a rest."

He turned to his mother, who wore a dark expression. "How is she doing, really?"

"I'm sure she is worried about all of you. The grief is taking time to ease. She did the same thing when Hank was here a few weeks ago."

Zeke put his hand on Tom's shoulder. "Since Pam's off today, why don't you take her home, so she can get ready for tonight? Then you can help set up the stage."

As they got into the station wagon and started into the street, Tom turned to Pam. "You know, I've seen the effect of death with the squadron, but being out there, you never think about how it affects the family at home. Death becomes a part of life there. Soldiers come and go."

Pam picked at her skirt. "You mean you don't feel anything for the ones who are killed?"

"Sweetheart, there are so many of them, I guess it numbs us. Seeing Jenny so upset gives me a different view of it. When I made my first kill, something happened to me." He was silent for a moment. "I know the enemy has family at home, too, but we're trained to think of them as not human. They're Japs and they need to die. I do know if I didn't kill them they would kill me. I imagine they are told the same thing."

As he parked in front of her house, Pam put her head on his shoulder. "You have changed, but war changes everyone."

He put his fingers on her cheek, and she looked up at him with such love he felt the warmth spread over him, and he kissed her with more desire than he'd ever known. He cupped her face. "I'll pick you up at six."

Pam gave him a small smile. "I'll be ready."

While he drove back to the theater, he pondered the thoughts this incident with Jen put in his mind. *I'm not the same person who left here a few years ago. Can I go back to where I was after the war is over? They tell me this is what I'm fighting for, but will my whole outlook on life ever be the same?*

****

Pam applauded loudly along with the rest of the audience as the cast came out for their final bows, Emily and Dave together in the center of the stage accepting all the "Bravos" with shining smiles.

Tom leaned toward Pam. "Little Em has really turned into a star."

Pam nodded. "She and Dave put in a wonderful performance. Still, it must have been hard for your parents to pull back for them."

"I think my mother is secretly proud of her, but the competitive actress in her is jealous."

As the audience headed toward the exits, Tom latched onto Pam's arm and they made their way across the stage and into the wings, where they were caught up in the huge celebration of cast and crew taking place. Even Jenny had a smile as she hugged her father, congratulating him.

When finally the jubilant crowd had quieted

down to a low hum, they heard a loud rapping near the stage. Standing by the entrance to the dressing rooms was a familiar-looking couple. Emily gasped. "It's George Burns and Gracie Allen—Oh, my stars! They were out in the audience?"

Burns and Allen glanced at each other and George grinned. "Are the Shafer brothers around?"

Emily's eyes grew bigger. "And they know Dad and Uncle Josh?"

Josh came out of the crowd of stunned people, Zeke right behind him, with Josh offering his hand first. "So good to see you again."

Zeke smiled. "What brings you back to our neck of the woods?"

George took a puff of his cigar. "We were passing through with the USO and thought we'd see if the Golden North theater was still in business."

Coming up to them, Addy warmly greeted Gracie. "You two have certainly done well."

Gracie laughed. "I remember you, Addy. You gave quite a performance when we were here. Where is your son?"

Addy beckoned to Tom, and he and Pam came over. "This is the one who kept me from opening night, Tomas Shafer. Tom, George and Gracie were here the night you were born."

George shook his hand. "And in the army, too. We're here for you boys."

Tom acknowledged the support. "Thank you, sir." He turned to Pam. "This is my girl, Pam Wright."

In awe of the celebrities, Pam could only gulp a shy "Hello" as she shook their hands.

George turned back to the brothers. "We brought along a couple of the producers for the USO show, and they'd like to talk to you."

Josh took a deep breath. "Where are they?" he asked.

George gestured toward the lobby. "They're waiting out there."

"We'll see them in the office right away."

A murmur of excitement ran through the backstage group as Pam gripped Tom's arm. "I wonder what they want?"

Tom shook his head. "I'm not sure, but from listening to my parents talk about show biz, when producers want to talk to you, they may be interested in your product."

"You mean the musical?"

"I'm sure we'll find out."

Sure enough, at the opening theater season party for the cast and crew in the restaurant, there were two unfamiliar men at the main table with the Shafer families.

Josh stood and rapped his spoon against his champagne glass. "Attention, everyone! I want to introduce Mr. James Rodgers and Mr. Albert Simpson. They're the producers for the USO show that's headed to the army base in Anchorage. I'm sure most of you noticed George Burns and Gracie Allen backstage after the show."

All the attendees applauded.

"Well, George and Gracie were one of the first acts at the theater when we opened, and tonight they came back to visit us and brought Mr. Rodgers and Mr. Simpson with them. Mr. Rodgers would like to say a few words. Mr. Rodgers?"

A middle-aged man with a congenial smile took Josh's place. "First, I want to congratulate all of you for a smash show. I haven't seen such an original piece in a long time. Next, we talked to the Shafers about possibly taking this show to Broadway to see how it flies."

There was no sound in the restaurant as everybody stared slack-jawed at Mr. Rodgers. Then a spontaneous cheer went up.

He put both hands up to bring order to the crowd. "You may not hear anything for a few months, but I promise you, as soon as the USO tour is finished, we're going back to New York to work on it."

Knowing this must have been the biggest thing to hit the theater in a long time, Pam was glad to see Jenny smiling and hugging her parents. *I know it will take time, but Jenny has a spirit that will help her through, along with her close family. The baby will give her a reason to go on, too.*

Pam looked around. Tom was over at the far end of the restaurant, talking to his brother, Scott, who was thinking about enlisting in the army after he graduated next year, and Pam's mind went back to the war.

Out of the radio came, "I'll be seeing you, in all the old familiar places..." *That song always makes me cry. I need some fresh air.* She went out to the lobby and grabbed her coat. The cold crisp breeze outside revived her as she leaned against the building. She opened her purse, pulled a cigarette from its pack, and lit it. A deep inhale, and then she watched the smoke swirl up into the night sky.

"Hello, beautiful!" she heard next to her and turned to face Vic Houston.

A wave of revulsion washed over her. "What are you doing here, and what do you want?"

An oily smile crossed his lips. "I'm on leave, too. And what do you think I want?"

Anger rushed through her. "Why are you always where I am? Are you following me? Stay away from me, Vic!" She threw the cigarette down and turned to the door.

Grabbing her arm, he said in her face, "I don't think so."

Wrenching her arm away, she opened the lobby door as Vic lunged toward her. "Stay away!" she shrieked just as Tom stepped out of the restaurant. He was across the lobby in a flash.

With a swing at Vic, knocking him down, he yelled, "What the hell are you doing?"

Vic, rubbing his jaw, glared at Tom. "I'm here to see Pam. You can't pull that rank crap on me here."

Pam yelled at Vic, "I don't want to see you! I don't want you following me around! I don't want anything to do with you! Leave me alone!"

"We'll see about that." Vic got up slowly, then jumped at Tom, throwing him off balance.

Zeke and Josh ran out from the restaurant, with Addy and Muriel behind them. Addy pulled Pam out of the way, while Zeke and Josh hung on to the two combatants.

Muriel hurried to the office. "I'm calling the sheriff."

Pam sobbed in Addy's arms, while the two boys glared at each other. Zeke kept a firm grip on his son, and Josh held Vic back. Vic turned a pleading eye on Josh. "I just wanted to talk to Pam."

Tom's eyes flashed. "She didn't seem to want to talk to you."

"That's because you've poisoned her mind against me."

A murmuring group gathered at the restaurant door, and Zeke noticed the curiosity. "Things are under control, folks. You can go back to the party."

Jenny and Muriel turned them back as Pam heard a car stop in front of the lobby doors. Sheriff Sam slid in between the blackout curtains and eyed the group. "Okay, what's going on here?"

Leaning on Addy, Pam related what had happened. Sam listened, watching Vic carefully. "Is it true that Miss Wright told you to stay away from her?"

Vic hesitated a moment. "She doesn't get how Shafer has her bamboozled."

Pam moved away from Addy and confronted Vic. "I have my own mind, Vic, and if anyone is poison, it's you! Sheriff, whenever he's in town, he seems to be following me around and spying on me." She whirled on Vic. "Was that you sneaking around our yard last October?"

He spread his hands out dismissively. "Now, whatever gave ya that idea, darlin'?"

The sheriff got close to his face. "Answer the lady's question. Were you in the Wright's yard last October?"

Vic turned a sneer on Pam. "No."

"Then what are you doing here now?" she shot back. "Why are you always where I am?"

"Because you're my girl."

"*I am not your girl!* I never was and I never will be!"

Putting his hand on Vic's shoulder, the sheriff moved him to the door. "I think it's time to move along here."

"You can't arrest me for talking to her!"

"No. But I can arrest you for a public disturbance. Now take my advice and go home. Leave the young lady alone."

Vic stood for a moment, staring at Pam. Tom growled, "Did you forget where the door is? Would you like for me to show you?"

Vic turned his eyes on Tom and gave a sloppy salute. "No, thanks, Mr. Officer, *sir.*" Then he stalked out.

Tom went to Pam and replaced his mother as her protector. Pam melted into his embrace and cried anew. Her misery knew no limits.

Zeke gave Tom the car keys. "Take Pam home. Don't let her walk to the door by herself."

Trembling in Tom's arms, Pam asked, "Sheriff, is there anything I can do? I feel like a prisoner."

Looking at his feet, the sheriff replied slowly, "I

know it isn't fair to you, but no laws have been broken. Just don't go *anywhere* alone."

After the sheriff left, Pam dried her tears. "I'm so sorry this happened. I didn't want to ruin your party."

Addy shook her head. "Don't blame yourself for this. From what I can see, you're not encouraging him. He's a very troubled young man."

Josh brought over their coats and hats. "Pam, you can be sure you'll be safe here. And I know your father will take care of things at your home."

Tom helped her into her coat, and she smiled at them all. "Thank you, so much." *They feel as much my family as my own. Are they doing this for me or for Tom?* She dismissed that last thought as silly.

Tom brought the car around, and as Pam slid into the passenger seat he took her hand and leaned in for a kiss. "I may not be here to protect you, but you can count on our families to look out for you."

As they drove past the alley beside the theater, Pam thought she saw a shadowy figure, but it disappeared as she turned to look. "Tom, I thought I saw someone in the alley."

Tom turned the car and moved up the driveway to the back of the building, catching the walls in the headlights. "Stay here. I'll check the other side of the alley." He took a flashlight out of the glove compartment. "Lock the door behind me."

She watched as he moved in and out between the buildings. He came back and she flipped the lock up again. "Well?" she asked as he settled in.

"I didn't find anything." He held her hand. "Don't worry. You'll be protected. I'll see to it." They continued to the Wrights's home with no further incident.

Chapter 10

My dear son,
I'm sorry, I haven't written for a while. I suppose Pam told you of the birth of Chase Marshall, Jr. Jenny has come out of her melancholy, thank heavens. He is a precious boy, and your Uncle Josh and Aunt Muriel are beside themselves with their first grandchild. The boy is going to be properly spoiled. The Marshalls are very proud of him, as well. As Clara says, Chase is still around in his son.
Mr. Rodgers and Mr. Simpson got back to us after their USO tour. They want your dad and Uncle Josh to go to New York to help set up the stage show of Gold Rush. Dan Hansen has agreed to direct it. It should open in late summer or early fall. Em and Dave are going to play the leads. I guess this old, aged actress is ready to be put out to pasture. Anyway, your Aunt Muriel and I will run things until they return. Maybe we can bring back the variety shows for a while.
Since the bartender, Charlie, has gone into the navy, Pam has taken over the job. She's very good at it. Vic hasn't showed after four months, so she has been able to relax. She and I like to take breaks and talk about how much we miss you. She's a brave girl, Tom, and tougher than you think. She reminds me a lot of myself at her age.
Take care, son. My prayers are with you.
Love,
Mom

Tom took a puff of his cigarette and exhaled, watching the smoke curl in the cool May air. Ken joined him outside the barracks, and Tom took the pack and shook one out for his friend. Ken fingered it before he lit it. "Calm before the storm, eh, pardner? What do you think of the new P-38 Lightning?"

Tom paused a moment. "It's a funny-looking plane, with that split tail, but I think they're easier to handle. With these orders, though, I want to enjoy today. There may not be another one for me after tomorrow."

"Ah, come on! The Japs lost a lot of planes on Guadal. I'll bet we outnumber them ten to one."

"That's very optimistic of you. Especially, if they get reinforcements before the battle."

"Well, it's up to us to see that doesn't happen. Just think, you need only one more kill for ace, and I need three. We should make that tomorrow. Those Japs should've thought twice before they attacked the good old U.S. of A."

Dropping the butt in the dirt, Tom put it out with the toe of his boot. "At least we have the country behind us. My family's theater always starts the movies with 'God Bless America,' and they've become a main stop for the War Bond tours."

"When I went home on leave a few months ago, my dad had just gotten another contract to sell our cattle to Defense. He says the military gets more of our beef than the family does. Hell, this past summer was the first that he knew of where we didn't have a steer on a spit for the Fourth of July."

The two boys were silent for a few moments. Then Tom spoke up. "Our theater and your dad's ranch sound good right now."

Ken put his cigarette out and slapped Tom's shoulder. "They're who we're fighting for. Let's go in and get some grub."

Later that evening, Tom stretched out on his bed, re-reading his last letter from Pam. Taking the small picture out of his pocket, he gazed at the image, wishing she were here with him. Since high school he had been able to discuss anything with her. Now he felt the distance that this war had caused. How he wanted to look into those eyes that resembled the deep blue of the ice in Glacier Bay, where they had traveled so many times. *I have to hang on for her. She's the most precious thing in my life right now.* He could almost smell her Evening in Paris perfume.

All too soon it was time to get up and report to mess. Tom had drifted to sleep with Pam's letter on his chest and her essence in his mind. Ken slapped Tom's feet. "Hey, pardner, you looked so peaceful there last night, I just peeled your boots off. Come on, it's oh-five hundred!"

Putting the letter on his nightstand, Tom deposited Pam's picture in his pocket. "Well, sweetheart, here we go," he said as he patted his shirt front. He pulled on his boots and joined Ken in the mess line.

Sitting on one of the long benches lining the tables, the boys set to work on their trays of scrambled eggs and sausages. Tom picked at his food, his stomach knotting up. *For some reason, I'm more nervous on this mission than I've been with the others. Mom always has feelings of foreboding before something bad happens, she says. Is that what's wrong with me? God, let me get through this day.*

Walking with Ken out to the tarmac, Tom extended his hand to his friend. "Buddy, good luck to both of us, and I hope we meet back here this evening."

Ken slapped Tom's shoulder. "Beat you to dinner tonight!"

Tom climbed into the P-38 Lightning and went through the procedures for starting and warming it up, as the other pilots did the same. He gave a wave to Ken, who returned it. Then Captain Allison's plane taxied to the runway, and the others pulled into line.

While waiting for the signal to take off, Tom gazed at Pam's picture. *Give me some of your strength, sweetheart. I'm going to need it.* He breathed out a sigh and, at the signal, took off into the clear air. The island quickly slipped away beneath him, and the sun shone with a dazzling light. He was grateful he was headed west this morning. The May days had many hours of daylight, so he suspected it would be a long fight.

The island of Attu was on the horizon, and it looked like a hell on earth. A day or so ago, the U.S. land forces had invaded from the north and south beaches, with the Japs putting up a whale of a fight. Dirt and dust, kicked up from countless shells from both sides, wafted into the air like brown smoke. The closer Tom flew, the better he could see men on the tundra, crawling around like ants on a hill.

A few miles ahead, Tom picked out what looked like Jap Brown Betty planes coming toward them. Over the radio, Captain Allison's voice called, "Split!" Quickly Tom and Ken pulled left with some of the 38's following them while others went right, to surround the Jap forces.

The experienced Jap pilots countered by pulling up or going down. As they did, Tom saw one turn sharply and fire. An agonizing jolt went through him. The Japs had the first kill. Tom and Ken ducked around a Betty, just out of range of the Jap's gun. Ken did a close skim over the enemy plane and, while the pilot was distracted, Tom pelted him with gunfire. The Betty's engine blew in a red-and-gold blast. Tom had reached his ace kill. Ken gave him a thumbs up, and they followed their next target.

With this pattern they went on through two more planes that Tom set up and Ken blasted. Tom waved at Ken and held up his index finger. *One more, buddy, and you get ace, as well.* Tom thought he and Ken could do anything.

Slicing through another plane, Ken glanced Tom's way. Ken's thumbs-up turned into a frantic wave and, too late, Tom turned to see a Jap on the other side of him. His plane shook from the impact of the Jap's bullets, the engine began to sputter, and a thread of smoke wove its way into the cockpit. *I've got to get out of here before the engine explodes!* Tom hit the latch on the slide, but it was jammed. Taking a breath, trying not to panic, Tom unbuckled the belt and hit the latch again. When it slid back, he was sucked out of the plane just as flames burst where he had been sitting moments ago.

Pulling the rip cord on his chute, Tom was jerked up into the air while his plane turned into a fireball that hit the water in pieces far below. The cuff on the right leg of his trousers was smoldering, so he rubbed his other leg over it until the embers were out. By this time, he had taken stock of where he was coming down—Attu, where the fighting forces were. At least he wouldn't be in the water.

I've got to try to maneuver toward our flags. If he landed on the Jap side, he would be dead for sure. When he was about a thousand feet above the ground, bullets started whizzing past him. *Damn, I'm a sitting duck!* He heard a plane swoop down and strafe where the firing seemed to be coming from. Bullets ceased to fly. *Thank you, Ken, my friend.*

Tom floated to a small ridge above the ocean. It was near one of the troop landings, with vegetation trampled all over the area. The chute billowed out as he touched the ground and started loosening the bindings.

He tried to get his bearings, dropping to the ground just in case there were more snipers around, although it looked like the battle had moved on from there some time ago. He scuttled behind a small mound and peered through the tufted grass, noticing the path the troopers had taken. His throat was dry and, taking a gulp of water from his canteen, he felt the liquid go all the way down to his stomach. *I don't have a weapon, so I'd better stay low.*

Muscles tightened as he inched his way along. Suddenly there were several shots fired behind him. The chute had fluttered in the sea breeze and someone had aimed at it. *I've got to keep going. The chute must've acted like a decoy. That should give me time to find a way out of here.*

Five hundred feet from where he'd landed, by his reckoning, several forms lay hidden in the grassy slope. As he crawled toward them, they took on grotesque shapes, and he realized they were dead soldiers. *Those are American army uniforms. At least I'm following the right side. Maybe there are guns I could use.*

As he got closer, he noticed a captain's uniform on one. The wind brought the metallic odor of blood and the sweet sickly smell of excrement to his nose. He rose a little to creep to the body, and froze in horror. The captain had sustained a gut shot, and his intestines were beside him like a pile of bluish sausage links. Bile came up in Tom's throat and he vomited into the grass.

Shaking his head to clear it, he eyed the body for a weapon and saw a pistol strapped to the captain's belt.

I've got to do this.

He stepped around the viscera, unsnapped the holster, and pulled out the gun. Holding his breath, he checked the captain's jacket pockets, found two extra clips, and slipped the ammo into his pocket before he rolled down the hill. At the bottom, he put the pistol down next to him on the grass and sat with his head in his hands, fighting his stomach.

Finally, when he could suck in a deep breath, he checked the clip in the gun; it was fully loaded. Saying a quick prayer for the dead men, he took another swig of water, slipped the pistol under his belt, and went on his way again.

A half-hour later, he heard the rat-a-tat of machine guns and knew he was coming up onto the front. The top of a ridge gave him a view of Americans down below, engaged with the Japs by the American compound.

At a noise behind him, Tom whipped out the gun, turned fast, and fired when he saw the Japanese uniform. The man had been wounded earlier and couldn't get his rifle up in time; it discharged into the ground as blood spilled from his chest where Tom's bullet had hit him, a sickening sight. In training for air combat, pilots were trained to kill planes, and although they had to learn how to kill soldiers in case of ground combat, they never had to watch a pilot die.

Tom turned back to the ridge and calculated how to get down to the American troops with as much cover as he could. It looked like they held the beach, so he would head there, carefully keeping on the tramped path the Americans must have used.

The wind whipped around his head as he descended the cliff side, sometimes sliding on scree as he grasped the rough rocks. Returning to the tundra grass, he crept into a small valley where he could hear the thunder of the firing. *I must be close. I'd better take cover again.*

"Psst, Lieutenant!"

Tom whirled to see a small squadron of seven privates in an alcove of rocks. "Did you men get lost?"

"Sir, we lost all our officers, and we don't know what to do next."

There was anxiety in their eyes. Here were

soldiers, younger than himself, looking confused. Tom judged the area he had moved into. "Boys, keep along the line of the beach that dips down, so if you crouch, they won't see you. We should make it to the rear. How is your ammunition?"

"We've got enough, sir."

"Good. Follow me." These new recruits wouldn't have had the battle tactics he'd received in officers' training, but, being a pilot, he had never had to use his knowledge. *I guess I never really believed I'd be in this situation.* He prayed he remembered correctly and could get the soldiers to safety. He fingered the small square in his pocket. *Wish me luck, sweetheart.* He stepped out with the seven privates behind him.

Sand and dust seemed to be everywhere, kicked up by the steady ocean breeze and the explosions that roared in his ears. It was all he could do to keep his eyes clear as he and the men edged their way to the American troops' rear. Tom found himself breathing and spitting sand. Finally he spotted a major with his battalion on the stretch of beach. Sliding down the small rise, he saluted the major. "Sir, I found these soldiers without any commanders and brought them back."

"I'm grateful, Lieutenant," he said as he returned a salute. "Who are you? I'm Major Porter."

"Lieutenant Tomas Shafer, sir," he replied and went on to explain what had happened.

The major turned to the soldiers, lined up behind Tom. "Men, Colonel Jacobs is over in that tent. You can report to him."

One of the privates saluted the major. "Yes, sir." He turned to Tom. "Lieutenant Shafer, thank you, sir."

Tom smiled. "You're welcome—?"

"Private Abner Styles, sir."

"Private Styles, you can take charge now." Tom looked at the major. "If that's all right with you, sir."

At the major's nod, Styles snapped Tom a salute. "Yes, sir!" Turning to the others, he said, "Let's go!"

Just as Tom was about to ask the major for orders for himself, an explosion not far forward blew tundra grass and dirt all over them. Both dropped to the ground, hearing cries and screams from over the ridge. The American forces opened up with their answering fire, and the attack temporarily ceased. Tom and the major raised their heads slowly. "You up to seeing what happened, Lieutenant?"

"I'll help in any way I can, sir."

"Good. Come on!" The major carefully climbed up the rise and waved for Tom. "It looks clear of the enemy for the moment."

Tom scrambled up as medics ran from the other side of the beach. The ghastly panorama spread out in front of him. In the small valley where the troops had been before the attack, men lay covered in blood, with soldiers who had escaped harm hurrying to help them. The cliffs on the other side belched dark smoke from American grenades sparking fires where the enemy had been.

Putting nausea out of his mind, Tom helped get the casualties onto the medics' stretchers. He almost lost control when an arm came off in his hand. *God, if there's a hell, I'm in it.*

Major Porter put his hand on Tom's shoulder. "I think we got all the ones we can save, Lieutenant. We'll have to come back later for the dead. I just got word another troop of Japs is headed this way." Porter dropped over the side of the rise to the beach as the soldiers took position again.

Tom was about to follow when he heard, "Help me!" from a boulder on his right. He lurched there and sucked in a breath. A wounded soldier had his foot caught in a vee in the rock, but that wasn't what made Tom gasp—the wounded man was Vic. They stared at each other. *Oh, it would be so easy to leave*

*him here. He would be gone from Pam's life forever.
But Captain Allison said to take care of the men.*
Wrestling with his conscience took only a moment.

In a heartbeat, he took the pistol out of his belt. Vic's eyes widened, and Tom could smell the fear, until he used the butt of the gun to break one side of the rock vee and free Vic. Grabbing Vic by the arm, he practically threw him over the rise.

Suddenly Tom heard shots, and, as he jumped over to the beach, a spray of red bloomed above the knee of his trousers. Hitting the beach hard, Tom gritted his teeth against the burning sensation in his leg. An explosion nearby covered him with sand before he could get up, and as he wiped his face he saw a couple of medics hurrying toward him while two others took Vic away.

"Hold still, sir!" a young blond soldier said as he and his partner crawled over to Tom with a lightweight stretcher. The man who had spoken deftly used his knife to cut the trouser leg above the blood-soaked material. "It looks like the bullet went straight through. I'll need to make a tourniquet to stop the bleeding, sir."

Tom slid his belt out of its loops. "Here, use this."

"Thank you, sir." The battle noise stopped as the two men strapped Tom onto the stretcher and headed toward a tent under the shelter of the rocks. Every jostle brought a new agony of pain from his leg, but he held on. *God, get me through this.*

The tent was a makeshift hospital. Overworked doctors and medics scurried around like crazed mice, tending to the wounded. One of the harried doctors took a look at Tom's leg. "We have to get the bleeding to stop. Keep the belt tight for a few more minutes. I think we can take you in then." He went to check on someone else.

Tom gritted his teeth and held on, until

everything seemed to slow down. His breathing shallowed and sweat poured from every inch of skin, but he was freezing. Darkness flowed like a wave over him.

****

Pam tried to put it out of her mind that she hadn't heard from Tom in over a week. She knew there had been an invasion of Attu and, after nineteen days, the Americans had regained the island. She suspected that Tom was in that battle. *God, please let him be all right.*

The theater was chaotic with the Shafer brothers getting ready to go to New York. Emily and Dave were to be in the original cast as the leads, so they were on their way, too.

Only a few hours before the four bound to New York would board the plane to Seattle, Pam, Jenny, and Em were sitting in the restaurant, having one more gab session.

Bubbling over with excitement, Em exclaimed, "I've never been to New York in my life. Now, I'm going to star on stage! Can you believe it?"

"Don't let the lights of Broadway overwhelm you, Em," Jenny said as she rocked Chase in his buggy. "Come back to us the same sweet cousin and not a prima donna."

She gave Jenny an impish smile. "Me? Nah!"

Pam offered her a cigarette. "I don't think I'd be as calm as you. I'd be a nervous wreck."

Taking a drag, Em leaned close to Pam. "Confidentially," she looked around, "I am."

"How are you getting to New York?"

Putting her cigarette down in an indent of the ashtray, Em counted on her fingers. "We're flying to Seattle, then taking the Empire Builder to Chicago, switch trains, and go right on, into the Penn Central Station in Manhattan."

Jenny shook her head. "Having you all away is

111

going to put an extra load on my mom and Aunt Addy, but they have Ivan and Kata to help. Scott and Don are doing very well running the lighting and projector. It's a good thing Uncle James trained them so well, despite their complaints about the time it took."

Too soon, Zeke came in to get Em. "The taxi's here, Em. Let's go. Dave is going to meet us at the airport."

The girls rose, and Jenny picked Chase up. They followed Zeke and Em into the lobby and out the doors to the waiting cab. Addy, Muriel, and Josh were already outside. Pam stood back by the doors while the family said goodbye to each other. She should give them their privacy, but she couldn't look away. These people had become as dear to her as her own family.

There was something beautiful in the way the two women clung to their men. Jenny had said of her parents and her aunt and uncle that neither couple had ever been apart since their wedding day. The way they gazed at each other warmed Pam's heart. *I want Tom and me to have a love like that. No matter how long we're together, I'd want him to look at me with that deep love.*

Lost in her reverie, Pam heard Em. "I couldn't leave without saying goodbye to you." She threw her arms around Pam's neck. "I can't wait for the day you and Tom get married and I'll have a real sister!"

Pam smiled and hugged back. "Knock 'em dead in New York!" Em grinned and ran to the taxi. *Neither can I wait, Em.* Zeke and Josh returned her wave to her as they disappeared into the cab, and then she leaned against the building and waited for the three women to join her.

Jenny slipped her arm through Pam's. "Mother's going to watch Chase for a while. You and I can get set up for tonight."

With Amelia's help, the girls had the restaurant and bar ready to go in a couple of hours, while Ivan, Scott, and Don set up the movie in the projection booth. Pam and Jenny slipped out the back door to relax in the May sunshine and have a smoke.

They'd been out there about ten minutes when Addy and Muriel burst out the kitchen door, calling to them.

Jenny ran to her mother. "What happened?"

Muriel's face paled as she hugged her daughter. Addy took Pam's hand. "Pam, Jenny, we've received word that Tom has been wounded."

Pam's throat constricted. "What? How?" she rasped.

Addy put her arm around Pam as both of them shook, and sat on the steps with her. "From the information we have, his plane was shot down, and he parachuted into the battle. He was wounded and taken to the military hospital in Anchorage."

Pam swallowed hard. "Did they say anything more?" She searched Addy's face to find her answer.

"No. But they did say I could go there to see him. Come with me, Pam?"

Muriel spoke up. "We can take care of things here. Don and Scott can help out after school."

Pam hesitated. "Jenny will need—"

Jenny turned. "Go to him. He'll need you more." She took Pam's hands in hers. "Don't let me lose someone else I love." Tears shone in her eyes.

With her lower lip trembling, Pam said, "Believe me, I don't want to lose him, either."

Huffing, Addy stood up. "No more talk of losing anyone. Pam, be ready first thing in the morning. Maybe we can ride with your father to the airfield." At Pam's nod, she turned. "Muriel, I'll need to get a telegram to Zeke."

Muriel patted Addy's shoulder. "I'll do that now. I should be able to catch them at the train station in

Seattle."

"Good. Now, let's get back to work." With that, Addy marched into the building.

Muriel glanced at Jenny with a smirk. "She's starting to sound like Uncle Zeke."

When Pam's father picked her up that evening, she told him what had happened. "Can you take Mrs. Shafer and me to the airfield tomorrow morning? She booked us on the public transport plane to Anchorage."

He nodded. "Of course. I'm sorry to hear about Tom." He drew in a breath and blew it out slowly. "Stay as long as you have to."

"Thank you, Dad." Pam was filled with dread. *What am I going to find when I get there? Who am I going to find? Oh, Tom, please come out of this, for all of our sakes.*

The next morning, Pam climbed into the back of her father's Buick as Addy slid into the passenger seat. Her dad turned to Addy. "Give our good wishes to Tom when you see him. Let us know if there's anything we can do to help."

Addy nodded. "Thank you, Bill. Just keep Tom in your prayers."

He reached over and squeezed her hand. "You know we will." The rest of the trip passed in relative silence.

The transport was warming up on the tarmac as Pam and Addy faced it hand in hand. When Addy turned pale and started to tremble, Pam put her arm around her. "We'll face anything together when we get there."

Addy gave her an embarrassed half-smile. "I know that. It's just—" She gave a shuddering sigh. "I'm terrified of airplanes."

Pam looked at her in surprise. "We could have taken the ship."

Shaking her head, Addy retorted, "Too slow.

Shall we?"

The two women marched toward the plane. *I hope I can be as courageous as Mrs. Shafer.* Pam turned to wave at her father before she boarded.

After a harrowing flight for Addy, Pam helped the gray-faced woman into the terminal building. "Are you going to be all right?"

Addy eased herself onto one of the metal chairs. "Now I will be." She fanned her face with the ticket folder. "I don't know how Tom does it."

"Shall I find us a taxi?"

"Yes, we can get a room at the hotel, then go to the base hospital."

Pan secured a cab and helped Addy into it. After freshening up at the hotel, they headed toward the hospital, located in the middle of the busy compound. The noise of planes arriving and taking off was an almost constant din.

Addy went to the desk, where a young military nurse held court. She smiled up at Addy. "May I help you?"

"I'm Lieutenant Tomas Shafer's mother. I want to find out how and where he is."

The nurse turned to her switchboard, next to the desk, and plugged a cord into a numbered hole, flicking a lever next to the base of the cord. Picking up her headset, she spoke into it. "Lieutenant Shafer's mother wants to find out about him and wonders if she could see him...Yes, sir." She turned to Addy. "Major Camden, our chief surgeon, will be down here directly. Please have a seat." She waved her hand toward some wooden chairs at the side of the room.

A few minutes later, a tall man spoke to the nurse and she nodded in Addy and Pam's direction. Major Camden had arrived to tell them about Tom's condition and direct them to the ward.

Chapter 11

Tom remembered bits and pieces of the last few days, including the transfer to the hospital ship where doctors threw around encouraging words while he could tell his leg was in a splint. *Damn! If I hadn't stopped to help that no-account bastard Vic, I wouldn't have been shot.* He winced with every movement of the ship. The nurses gave him something for the pain, but there was a dull edge of it that never went away.

Opening the door to his ship ward, a doctor stopped at Tom's bed and picked up his chart from the metal foot rail. "I see you're awake, Lieutenant."

"Where are we going?" His voice was low and weak.

"You're on your way to Anchorage. You need surgery on that leg."

"What happened to it?" Alarm bells were going off in his head.

"The bullet you took went through above your knee, and some of the bone went with it. We need to put a rod and some screws in there to hold the ends of the thigh bone together."

Tom felt a sinking dread in his chest. "Will I be able to walk?"

The doctor watched him for a few seconds, then glanced back at the chart. "In a while, you should get most of your mobility back. Hospital time shouldn't be more than a month."

Tom sighed when he remembered that feeling of doom before the flight. Well, his mother was right. He must have gotten her instincts.

A couple of agonizing days later, Tom was taken off the ship, along with a few other serious cases. The orderlies tried to move him with the least jostling of his stretcher, but even with the painkillers he felt the ends of the bone in his leg rubbing together. They set four of the wounded in a waiting area inside the hospital building.

A salt-and-pepper-haired major came over. "I'm Major Camden, Chief Surgeon here. Let me take a look at that leg." He unwound the bandage from the splint.

Tom sucked in a breath when he saw how swollen his knee was, and he flinched at the pain when the major moved it slightly.

"Those medics at the front and on the ship stabilized it well. You were in good hands, Lieutenant Shafer." He motioned to one of the nurses. "Prep the lieutenant. I'll take him second."

A dark-eyed nurse, her raven hair pulled back in a tight bun, helped Tom out of his clothes. With a reassuring smile, she remarked, "Just relax. I do this all the time."

Tom's mouth twitched at the corners. "I don't."

Readying a syringe and needle, she tapped the air out of it. "This will help you before the surgery." After she gave him the shot, she patted his arm. "See you in recovery."

Tom was groggy for what seemed like several days. Finally, the ward full of wounded stopped disappearing as often as it came into focus, and Major Camden paid him a visit. "How are you doing, Lieutenant?"

"Head's clearing, sir. What did you do?" He peered at the pulley that supported his cast-covered leg.

The major looked at his chart. "We had to put a rod and screws in your thigh bone to hold the two ends together. The bullet took off a chunk of it."

Tom blew out a slow breath. "When can I go back, sir?"

"Not for a while. I had a talk with Major Raden—he's General Buckner's aide—and he'll be in to talk to you."

Tom put his head back on the pillow as the doc left. Flying was second nature to him now. *What am I going to do if I can't fly? If only I hadn't stopped to rescue Vic, I wouldn't be in this hospital bed. Damn him!* Tom gritted his teeth. *Vic probably got off with no more than a scratch.* Tom knew that as an officer he wouldn't be discharged from the army like a non-com with an injury, but they wouldn't let him go back to combat unless he was physically fit. *I wonder if they told my family yet? I sure would love to see them. And Pam, I hope she'll come up. I'd like to have news of the squadron. I pray everyone else came back safely.*

Later, while Tom was finishing lunch, a major came in, and Tom gave him a quick salute.

"Lieutenant Shafer, I'm Major Raden, here to deliver a message from General Buckner."

Tom shook the hand extended to him. "Yes, sir?"

"Lieutenant, we have a report from Colonel Jacobs about the battle on Attu. You seem to have made quite an impression on him."

"Did we—?"

"We drove the Japs out, and the island is secure." At Tom's nod, he continued, "We know that after you were shot down you not only made your way to the rear but you took several privates back with you, men we would have lost if they'd stayed where they were. Then you helped Major Porter with the wounded, and you rescued a trapped soldier before being wounded yourself. Is that right, Lieutenant?"

Hesitating a second, Tom replied, "Yes, sir."

"The colonel got in touch with your commanding

officer, and together they put in for a Purple Heart and a Bronze Star for you. Also, you have attained the rank of captain. There will be a formal ceremony when you're released from the hospital."

Tom glanced at him. "Will I be able to resume flying then, sir?"

With a smile, the major answered, "That will be up to the doc. We have a few weeks to work that out. In the meantime, Captain Shafer, concentrate on mending that leg."

"Thank you, sir." Tom saluted once more.

The next day, the doctor lowered Tom's leg from the pulley and let him move it around. "We don't want the leg muscles to atrophy, so you have to work them as much as possible. We'll give you crutches tomorrow, and you can go for a short walk."

Tom's painkillers were being cut back, so the leg was a little sore, but the discomfort was nothing he couldn't handle. Every day of this was a step closer to getting back into a plane, and getting up on crutches gave Tom a sense of freedom after being confined to bed for so long. Moving around allowed him to get acquainted with the other junior officers in the ward, but the greatest thing was not having to ask for a bedpan anymore; that had been humiliation.

A week after the surgery, Tom sat propped up in his bed, quietly reading the morning newspaper, when a bright ray of sunshine lit up the ward with her golden hair and sky-blue eyes. The beautiful vision headed right toward him. "Tom! Oh, Tom!" She latched her arms gently around his neck and gave him a careful kiss on his cheek, which changed when he turned his head and gave her a full kiss on the mouth. *Lord, she tasted sweet!* Then he glanced over her head and saw his mother pulling the side curtains closed between his bed and the others in the ward.

Mom gave him a half-smile. "You don't want to make the others jealous."

Tom looked around. "Where's Dad?"

"He left with Uncle Josh and Em and Dave for New York before we heard about you being shot down. Aunt Muriel sent him a telegram. What happened? The army doesn't give out much information. We didn't know what we would find." Her voice wavered at the end as she drew over a chair next to them. Tom moved over, and Pam sat on the bed. He told them what he could about the battle and since, leaving out the fact that the soldier he'd helped was Vic. His mom and Pam gazed at him, glowing with pride.

When Tom noticed his mother was pale, although some color was coming back into her face, he asked, "Mom, are you all right?"

Gazing at her hands, she nodded. "Now, I am. We just arrived here by air."

His mouth gaped open. "You set foot in an airplane? You said something about a goon's age when I offered to take you up a couple of years ago."

Sighing, she said, "I didn't want to take the time to go by ship. I was worried about you."

Pam squeezed his hand. "She used both of our airsick bags on the way over."

At Tom's chuckle, his mother added, "We're going home by ship, of course."

A clomping of boots on the linoleum floor made Tom look up as a familiar face peered around the curtain. "Ken! You old dog! You made it through. What are you doing here?"

Ken shook Tom's hand. "I had a few days' leave, so I thought I'd see how you were. But you have company—"

"That's all right." Tom made the introductions. "Ken saved my skin when I went down. The Japs were shooting at me, and he strafed them. I didn't get a chance to thank you, buddy."

Mom put a hand on Ken's shoulder. "We all thank you."

"Shucks, ma'am, Tom would have done it for me."

Tom looked steadily at Ken. "What happened?"

With a grim line to his mouth, he replied, "We wiped them out. They fought to the last man, and at the end a few were captured and the rest committed suicide. I've never heard of anything like it."

Pam shook her head. "Those people are fanatical, and that's why this war scares me. Both the Nazis and the Japs seem to be power-mad."

Interlacing his fingers with hers, Tom said seriously, "That's why we have to defeat them."

Ken gazed at Tom's cast. "When did the doc say you'd be ready to fly again?"

Some of that frustration came over Tom. "I should know in three weeks. I tell you, Ken, if it wasn't for stopping to help—that soldier, I wouldn't have gotten shot."

Ken hesitated, then sighed. "Well, you never know." Putting his hand on Tom's shoulder, he said, "Hope to see ya back. You have lovely company, so I'll hightail it out of here." With a tip of his cap, he bowed. "Ladies."

Pam nodded. "It was a pleasure to meet you, Ken." Mom agreed.

After he left, a male nurse came in. "Captain, it's time for your walk." Turning to Pam and Mom, he advised, "You can wait for him in the atrium. That's downstairs to your right. He has to get out twice a day on the crutches."

Mom gave Tom a kiss on the cheek. "We'll be waiting. Come on, Pam, there must be somewhere we can get coffee."

Tom reluctantly watched the two walk away as the nurse gave him a robe and helped him swing his leg off the bed. A growing concern in his gut bothered him. *What if I can't get back to flying? What earthly good will I be to anyone? Since I started flying, it's all I ever wanted to do.* He gave a resounding crack to the plaster cast with his fist—and immediately reacted to the pain in both his hand and his leg.

****

Taking their steaming cups from the cafeteria to the sunny atrium, Pam and Addy looked around. A number of brown wicker chairs with light green cushions were interspersed with potted plants that made the room seem like a terrible garden. Wounded and sick soldiers sat in various seats or in wheelchairs, soaking in the warmth of the day. Addy pointed to a couch and a coffee table by one of the windows, and they sat down to wait.

After just a sip of her coffee, Addy set it on the table. "Tom seems to be himself, but there's something wrong, and I can't put my finger on it."

Pam's stomach gave a slight twist. She had been thinking the same thing. "Of course, he's been through a horrible experience. That's sure to affect him some way."

"I don't know if you caught it, but that nurse called him 'Captain.' He didn't tell us they gave him a promotion."

"You're right. I wonder if there's anything else he didn't say." Pam watched as Tom worked his way to them, managing the big plaster cast, his rubber crutch tips making sucking sounds on the hard floor. The male nurse drew one of the chairs close and helped Tom sit, then gently raised Tom's leg to rest on the table.

"Would you like some coffee, Captain?"

"No, thank you."

"Then I'll come back for you a little later." At Tom's nod, he departed.

Addy pursed her lips. "Why didn't you tell us you're now a captain?"

Hesitating, Tom stared out the window. "Didn't cross my mind."

An orderly came over with an envelope. "Telegram for you, Captain."

Tom opened it as the man stepped away. "It's from Dad: 'Tom, heard news. Waiting for train in Seattle. Get well. From all. Dad.'" Waving his hand to the orderly, he said, "Would you send a reply for me, please." The man took out a pad of paper and pencil, and Tom continued, "On the mend. Don't worry. Tom."

"Yes, sir!" The man saluted and went on his way.

Pam moved to the arm of Tom's chair, putting her fingers on his shoulder. "What's bothering you?"

"Besides the damn war?" he snapped. Withdrawing her hand, Pam stood. Taking it again and kissing it, Tom sighed. "I'm sorry, sweetheart. I feel so useless here. If I hadn't been so careless, I wouldn't have been shot down."

Addy glared. "Don't start blaming yourself for the accident. At least you're alive. The army wouldn't raise your rank if they thought you'd done anything wrong."

"I have a feeling in my gut that I'm not going to fly in this war again. I'm going to get a desk job or some such nonsense, because of my leg."

"Listen, boy, you've paid quite a price to fight against the Japanese. You have absolutely nothing to be ashamed of. If you have to work a desk job, so be it! They need everyone working to defeat the enemy."

"That's easy for you to say! I won't be in the ranks of the victorious soldier or the honored dead. I've joined the ranks of the maimed, and all I get for that is jewelry!"

Pam glanced sadly at him. "You're feeling sorry for yourself that you can't be bathed in glory in an office. Tom, I can't believe you're so selfish."

"You'll never understand."

Addy took Pam by the arm. "Come on. Let's go home. We're not needed here."

Looking back at Tom, Pam retorted, "But—"

Addy looked hard at her, with a glint in her eye. "I know what I'm doing."

Tom stared out the window as the two women left the hospital, and Pam pulled up as they went out the front door. "What's going on here?"

Hesitating a moment, Addy replied, "I haven't seen Tom sulk like this since he was thirteen, but he gets in these moods if things aren't going his way. The way I take care of it, I just walk out on him and let him brood. When he's over it, he'll let me know."

Pam drew back. "But if we go home—"

"We're not going home. We're going back to the hotel to wait for his call. You see, I left the hotel business card on the stand by his bed." She winked at Pam. "I know my son."

Their taxi arrived at the Anchorage Hotel fifteen minutes later, and when they walked into the lobby, with its frontier theme, a desk clerk stopped them. "Are you Mrs. Shafer?" At Addy's nod, he continued, "We had a call come in for you. If you want to wait here, I'll call back for you."

A small smile played around her lips. "Thank you, we will." They sat on one of the white overstuffed couches. "It took less time than usual. When you two get married, remember: that's the way to handle Tom when he gets in one of these moods."

Pam felt a rush go through her, thinking of marriage to Tom. "That's good to know. Thank you for telling me." Inwardly, she knew with a positive glow that she was accepted as a member of the family.

The clerk returned. "I have Captain Shafer on the line."

Going to the phone on the far end of the desk, Addy picked it up. "Hello?...I know it's been tough on you...uh-huh...Okay, we'll stay a few more days, if you promise to behave yourself...All right. Bye. Love you!" Addy placed the phone receiver back on its cradle. "We'll go back after dinner."

Pam shook her head. "That looked easy enough."

Addy chuckled. "I guess he's maturing. He isn't as stubborn as he used to be."

Pam couldn't wait to get back to Tom. She plowed through her dinner and tapped her foot while Addy paid for the meal. As the taxi dropped them off at the hospital, she was ahead of Addy going into the ward.

Tom smiled and held out his arms, and Pam settled into them. Addy pulled the side curtains again and sat on the chair. He flushed. "I'm sorry I acted like that. I guess when I saw Ken it hit me that my active days might be over. It's hard to think they might not let me fly anymore."

Interlacing her fingers with his, Pam kissed him. "I want you to come home safe." She sighed. "Purely selfish reasons, of course." Gazing into his incredible eyes, she saw a warm fire.

"Well, I happen to agree..." Pam heard Addy speaking, but the words faded into the distance while fireworks went off between her and Tom. "...and Glinda the Good Witch told me to tap my heels three times and say, 'There's no place like home.'"

Both Pam and Tom looked up and said, "Huh?"

Addy folded her arms. "I thought I was talking to myself." She waved off the apologies. "I know when I'm the fifth wheel. I think I'll go for a walk and let you two make googly eyes at each other."

Watching her disappear around the curtain, Pam whispered, "That was rude of us."

Tom touched her lips with his fingers. "Yes, it was." As he kissed her firmly on the mouth, she melted. The only thought in her head was that she was with Tom and he was alive. She wanted to keep him that way, and if that meant he had to take a ground job, he had to deal with that.

Later, while they were talking, a major stopped by. Tom sat up straighter. "Major Raden."

The major returned Tom's salute. "Captain Shafer. I have your orders here. A week after your release from the hospital, you are to report to McChord Field in Tacoma for your new assignment. General Buckner feels you would be perfect for training our new pilots, since you know how to fly most of the planes."

Tom's eyes lit up. "You mean I don't have to sit behind a desk, sir?"

Raden smiled. "The best place for an experienced pilot like you is in the air."

Tom saluted with a grin. "Thank you, sir. You don't know what this means to me."

After Raden left, Pam embraced Tom. "I'm so happy for you. I know this is what you love doing."

When Addy came back, they both informed her of the new job. Pam was relieved that Tom was now looking forward to his new assignment. The news had definitely cheered him up.

Chapter 12

Dear Son,

I am so proud of you. I wish I could be there for the ceremony, but we're right in the middle of getting ready for opening night. I know, from your last letter, you hope this will be a success for us. Dan Hanson is doing a great job of pulling the cast together. The producers have been peppering the town with one-sheets about the coming show.

The news that you're being transferred to McChord Field to train the new army pilots sounds like a great adventure. I know how much you love flying, and this will give your leg a chance to heal. You were upset not to get back with your squadron, but you must understand the army needs combat pilots who are fit. Maybe when your leg heals completely they'll let you into combat again.

Uncle Josh heard from Hank that he and Joe were going to try to make the ceremony. The navy there has just been put on watch where he's stationed, he said. Anyway, give our love to the family. We here miss all of you.

Dad

Standing in front of the small mirror in the bathroom, Tom wiped the rest of the shaving cream off his face. In the few days since his discharge from the hospital, he had been staying in one of the visiting officer's rooms. He had his papers waiting for the transfer to Tacoma and had resigned himself to the fact that he wouldn't go back to combat for a while. He might as well not brood about it.

Picking up the two canes leaning against the

white-tiled wall, he forced his leg to move. *By God, I'm going to get this leg working perfectly again, no matter what.* Tom went every other day to physical therapy, and despite the agony he was making the muscles move. At least he was off the crutches.

He made his way to the bed, where the dress uniform was laid out, clean and pressed. His knee, still stiff and scarred, bent slowly when he sat on the chair next to the bed. Painfully, he managed to dress himself. Every little bit of effort was a major victory for him.

A knock on the door made him jump. "MacGowen, is that you?" he asked, thinking it was the lieutenant who had been assigned to him as an aide.

"Nope."

I know that voice as well as my own. With a quick hobble, he reached the door and swung it open. "Hank! Joe! How did two tars like you manage to get into an army building?" He let his canes drop as he embraced his cousin and his friend.

Hank smirked. "We just told the guards there was a fight around at the back of the building."

Tom hit him on the back. "Okay, wise guy. I'll see you in a zoot suit yet."

Hank held his arm out, palm up. "Well, beat me, daddy, eight to the bar!"

Tom slapped his hand over Hank's. "Ha!"

Starting to laugh, Joe shook his head. "I would never take you two for hep cats, dressed like that." They all leaned on each other for a well needed laugh. Joe retrieved the two canes. "I see you're off the crutches already."

Tom walked himself around the room. "I'm bound and determined to get my leg back to normal, regardless of what the doc says. Who all is here? Have you seen the family?"

Hank nodded. "Our mothers, Jenny, and Pam

are here, but my mom and Jenny are going back by plane to Juneau this afternoon. It seems the theater and restaurant have been busy again. Your mother said she and Pam will stay until tomorrow. I heard you're going down to McChord."

"I guess they liked me so well when I trained there they want me to train the new pilots coming in."

Patting Tom on the shoulder, Joe grinned. "Well, who else knows how to fly any plane? I hear they have them all, there."

A certain excitement made its way through Tom's mind. "Maybe it won't be so bad, stuck in Tacoma."

Hank laughed. "Hell, Joe, maybe we should both shoot ourselves in the foot and sit at a desk, too."

Tom winced at that, but joined the others in their merriment. A young lieutenant rapped on the open door's jamb. "Captain, it's about time we get down to the field." He seemed surprised to see two navy men with Tom.

"MacGowen, could you drop these two at the viewing stands on the way out to the field?" Smiling at the man's confusion, Tom made the introductions. "Lieutenant, this is my cousin and this is my best friend."

The lieutenant saluted. "Yes, sir."

With a return of the salute, the little group headed outside to the Willys jeep parked out front. Joe helped Tom into the front seat while the lieutenant climbed behind the wheel. The two navy men jumped into the back.

The late June sunshine warmed their faces. Anchorage was going into the Alaskan summer with its almost endless day. Every Stars and Stripes on base was whipping in the fresh ocean breeze against the dark blue northern sky, snapping in unison as if ordered to do so by the brass.

The lieutenant stopped the jeep by the stands, and Hank and Joe exited the vehicle, scanning the stands until Hank pointed up into the right side. "There they are!" The boys started up the steps to their seats next to the family.

When they got to the line of honorees, McGowen helped Tom out. With the canes, he hobbled his way to the end. A few minutes later, all were assembled, and General Buckner took the stand. "We are here this morning to honor these fine young men whose heroics are helping to win this war on both fronts. Their bravery under fire is exceptional, and we would be remiss if we didn't acknowledge it. Please, reserve your applause till the end. Thank you."

The general started down the long line with a couple of his aides carrying the boxes of medals behind him. He personally pinned the honors to the men's uniform jackets and shook their hands. When he reached Tom, he nodded. "Captain Shafer."

Resting one of the canes against his leg, Tom saluted. "Yes, sir."

The general returned the salute. "I have for you the Purple Heart for being wounded and a Bronze Star for bravery in combat." He attached both to Tom's uniform and extended his hand. "Congratulations, Captain." Tom did feel proud of his accomplishment in battle after all. This was quite an honor.

When his hand was free, Tom saluted again. "Thank you, sir."

After the last recipient, the general turned toward the stands. "Let's say thank you to these brave boys." He led the applause that seemed to resound all around them. "Company dismissed." And the stands emptied out onto the field.

Outdistancing the rest, Pam planted a victory kiss on Tom's lips. He was only vaguely aware of the others coming up around him, until his mother and

Aunt Muriel turned weepy as they made over him and the medals. Jenny smiled and handed him his new cousin, Chase, who was dressed up in a little khaki outfit and promptly started crying at leaving his mother's arms for a stranger's.

Tom laughed and handed him back. "I guess there will be time for him to get to know Cousin Tom later."

Hank chucked Chase under the chin, which caused pouty lips. "Don't worry, he reacted the same to his Uncle Hank. You're in good company." Hank then compared Purple Hearts. He had gotten his in a ceremony on board ship.

Joe gave Addy and Muriel each a hug. "I guess my folks are watching things while you're here, right?"

Muriel nodded. "I don't know what we would do without them. But Jenny and I have to get back there tonight. Seems the longer this war gets, the more people come to the movies."

Addy sighed as she embraced Tom. "Let's hope the war won't last that much longer. We can use the business, but not the horror."

Tom spoke up. "Say, there's a café not far from here. Shall we go get some lunch?"

Slapping Tom on the back, Hank said, "Joe and I have to get back to the ship," and the boys said their goodbyes and left.

Muriel checked her watch, pursing her lips. "Jenny and I have a few hours before we leave. Should we call for a taxi? I think there are several out in front of the gates."

MacGowen pulled up in the jeep. "Where to, Captain?"

Thinking for a moment, Tom leaned toward the lieutenant. "We want to go to the Seaside Café." Turning to his guests. "Do you four girls think you can ride in the back of the jeep?"

Addy glance at it skeptically. "It would be a tight fit."

Putting his arm around Pam and looking down at her, Tom smiled. "Maybe you could sit on my lap?" Heat prickled at the thought.

Pam eyed him. "What about your leg?"

"It's strong enough to hold you."

Opening her mouth to say something else, Pam apparently changed her mind. Muriel held Chase while Addy and Jenny climbed in, then after transferring the baby to his mother Muriel got in, as well. MacGowen helped Tom into the front seat, and Tom drew Pam onto his lap. Lord, she smelled fresh and sweet, and how beautiful she was in her summer print dress. He wished the two of them were going back to his room instead of to lunch with the family, but first things first.

When they arrived at the eatery, Tom was grateful that his dress jacket covered to just below his hips. Pam seemed to be aware of the hard lump, because she gave him a wicked grin when she hopped out. *I can't seem to be around that girl without being aroused.*

Everyone chatted over lunch about everything that had happened since they'd been together last. MacGowen came back for them in an hour, and Tom insisted they take Jenny and Muriel to the airfield. By this time, Tom had managed to get a giggle out of Chase as he gave him back to Jenny and kissed and thanked her and her mother for coming.

Tom stood with his arms around his mother and Pam as they watched the airliner take off.

He glanced at his mother. "Are you—?" He pointed to the plane.

"You must be joking! We're taking the Alaskan sealiner to Juneau." Mom sighed. "It'll be another twenty-some years before I make that mistake again."

On the way back, Tom turned around to the women in the back. "We're going to have a special dinner tonight at the O club, and there's a dance at one of the hangers. Interested?"

Mom looked from Tom to Pam, then back again, with a smile pulling at the corners of her mouth. "I'll take the dinner, but I won't intrude on a son's date. Anyway, I don't think your dad would approve if a young handsome soldier picked me up. Although, how on earth are you going to dance?"

Tom chuckled at that. "There's no law that says I have to dance. We can sit and listen to the music. I can have MacGowen drop you off at the hotel after dinner. I'll see to getting Pam back later."

Pam had a trace of concern. "You can't drive, can you?"

MacGowen spoke up. "I can get you back, as well."

After their festive dinner, Tom told his mother, "I'll be at the docks to see you two off tomorrow."

She put her hand on his cheek. "I'm so proud of you." She turned to Pam. "Have fun at the dance tonight." With that, she left with MacGowen.

Tom gave Pam a kiss. "Want to head over to the hangar?"

Drawing back, she had a doubtful face. "Will you be able to walk that far?"

He grinned. "It's just across the road," he said, pointing to a large building with the double doors opened all the way.

Taking one of the canes, Pam put her arm around him. "Lean on me." With his puzzled look, she added, "I'm strong enough to help you over there."

A war was going on inside Tom. This wasn't how he thought a man should be. A man should have a woman depend on him, not the other way around, but he did have her arm around his waist. Maybe this wasn't so bad. Her flowered dress fluttered in the breeze and he loved the way her body moved against him. Before he knew it, they were at the hangar, and the raucous music of the band reached them with "Song of India" reverberating to the rafters.

Helping him sit at a small table near the doors, Pam squeezed his shoulder. "We can listen to the music from here. I'll get us something to drink. What would you like?"

Tom shook his head. "No, I'll get something."

She gripped his shoulder, tighter. "Rest your leg. I'll get us each a beer, how's that?" and she moved through the crowd to the bar. A few minutes later, a cold brew was in front of him.

Tom took a sip. "This sure won't be a good date. I can't dance with you."

Touching his arm gently, she smiled. "We're together. That's enough for me."

A couple of hours of listening to music and enjoying light conversation did him a world of good. Pam had even made sure they were near the cans, so he wouldn't have to travel far. Pam rose and leaned toward him. "I'm going to pick up something special for us." She disappeared into the crowd.

Tom jumped as someone leaned over his shoulders and gave him a hug. "Hello, darling. I thought that blonde would never leave."

Gasping with surprise, he watched a feminine form come around to caress his face and he looked into the green eyes of Mary Casey. "What the hell are you doing here?"

Her lower lip went into a pout. "That's not a nice greeting, but I think I can forgive you. I was here to honor the honorees. So to speak."

Tom steamed. "That blonde is the love of my life."

"Really? I didn't see any rings on either of you.

And you fascinate me." She put her fingers on his lips and kissed him.

Suddenly he heard glass breaking behind them. As he turned he saw Pam watching them, stricken-faced, with what was left of champagne glasses at her feet and a bottle in her hand.

Slamming the champagne down on the table, Pam pulled Mary away by the back of her uniform. "What do you think you're doing?"

Tom froze. This was way out of his experience with Pam. He'd never thought of someone fighting over him. That's what men did for women, not the other way around, right?

Twisting out of Pam's grasp, Mary gathered herself. "Just seeing an old friend."

"In my book, that would be a 'Hi, how are you,' without the tentacles." Glancing at the uniform shirt, Pam pointed at the neck. "You missed a few buttons."

Mary gave her a half-smile as she straightened her clothing. "Well, aren't you a cute child. What Tom needs right now is a woman."

Pam hauled off and slapped her. "How dare you tell me what Tom needs. You don't even know him."

Tom didn't know if he should step in. Neither of his parents had prepared him for this.

Rubbing her cheek, Mary hissed, "I know more about men than you do, honey. I'll stand back and let you fail. Then we'll see who knows him better." She sashayed back into the crowd.

Tom rose and hugged Pam. "I'm sorry. I didn't even know she—Mary—was here."

"That was the Mary Casey you told me about?"

He winced. "Yes. I never should have gotten involved with her. I can't believe what a tramp she is." The band started playing "Moonlight Serenade" and Tom and Pam swayed in time with the music. "I wish I could dance with you." He buried his face on

135

her neck and nibbled while sparks descended down his insides.

She kissed his ear. "This is nice, but should we be doing this here?"

Drawing back, he grinned at her. "Tell you what. Why don't you go find MacGowen, and we'll take this champagne back to my room."

With another kiss full on the mouth, Pam disappeared into the dancers on the floor. A couple of minutes later, she returned with MacGowen in tow, and Tom wondered if she was feeling the effect of the beers she'd had. Pam never was this forward before.

MacGowen saluted. "The lady here says you want to go to your quarters. Is that so, sir?"

Tom returned the salute. "Yes, Lieutenant, could you drop us at the building? Then you can go back to the dance for a while."

"What time do you want me to take the lady to the hotel?"

He checked his watch. "Eleven o'clock?" Glancing at Pam, she nodded. "That will give you three hours. Please be reasonably sober."

MacGowen saluted again. "Yes, sir." He turned to bring the jeep to the entrance.

Tom gazed at Pam's face as they waited. Her emotions, for once, were entirely unreadable. He put his hand on the small of her back as the jeep pulled up. MacGowen helped Tom into the front seat, and Pam climbed into the back. Glancing at the building before they left, Tom saw Mary watching on the arm of a major. *Looks like she wasn't lonely for long.* Mary gave Tom a small shrug as the jeep pulled away.

At his quarters, Tom had MacGowen's assistance out of the vehicle and then leaned on Pam as they walked to the door. Once in his room, Pam set the champagne on the table, and Tom kissed her passionately. Pointing to his left, he asked, "Could you get two glasses from that cabinet over there? I'm sorry they aren't the proper stem ones."

Pam smiled. "It'll probably taste the same." Coming back with the tumblers, she set them on the table as Tom popped the cork. The bottle's contents gurgled into the glasses while Pam sat across the table from him.

He raised his champagne in a toast. "Here's to us, and may this war be over soon." They clinked their glasses, and the bubbly liquid sparkled down his throat.

Closing her eyes as if to savor the swallow, she murmured, "Very nice. I hope it mixes with the beer well. I'm feeling very lightheaded." As she set her drink down, she sighed. "I'm afraid this war is going to go on forever." When he looked into her eyes again, there were tears nestled in the corners.

He rose and made his way around the table. "Here, now. Champagne is supposed to make you happy." He cupped her face. "Let me see the girl I love."

The corners of her mouth pulled up as she stood. "Mary was right. You need a woman tonight." Giving him a kiss that curled his toes, she murmured, "Let me be the woman you love."

"Pam—?"

Unbuttoning his dress jacket, she moved her hands over his shirt. "I love you too much to let anyone else be your woman."

The blood rushed to his groin, and a moan escaped his lips. This wasn't the girl he knew, but instinct took over as he moved his hands down the sides of her body and over her hips as she pressed close against him and moved his jacket to the chair. The evening sun flowed through the window and her golden hair shone like a halo as his fingers ran through it. He showered kisses down her neck, from her ear to her collarbone, while little sounds of arousal slipped from her throat.

"If you're having second thoughts, stop me now," he said, rubbing his erection against her.

As an answer, she unzipped the back of her dress and let it fall to the floor. "No second thoughts. Do you have—you know?"

He stopped for a moment. "Ah, yes." Grabbing his wallet, he pulled out a packet. "They issue these to us."

As they finished undressing each other, both reveled in the new sensations. When the last scrap was shed, they looked at each other with both underlying embarrassment and awe. Pam touched him with wonder, and he almost lost control but managed to collect himself as she helped him to the bed. When she ran her fingers over the scarred knee, she gazed at him with sadness in her eyes, but he laid the small packet next to him and took her arm, drawing her over. As they lay side by side. His hands cupped her breasts, and her nipples grew tight under his palms. Tom's dreams hadn't even come close to having her beside him like this. He opened the packet and slipped the rubber on.

"Will this be too painful for your leg?"

"No. I can put my weight on the other leg." He kissed her thoroughly. "Don't worry about me," he said with a rasp.

Pam lay on her back with a single tear coursing down her cheek. "You know I haven't done this before."

Tom nodded as he carefully hitched himself over her. "I'll be as gentle as I can." Gritting his teeth as he felt her slick opening, he moved his tip against it. Then, taking a deep breath, he thrust into her. Pam gave a small cry and wrapped her legs around him. She was soft, tight, and warm, and Tom quickly spent himself. He hit his forehead with the heel of his hand. "Damn. Damn. Damn."

Pam's lower lip started to tremble. "Did I do something wrong?"

Tom's heart went out to her. "No. I—" Rolling off her, he sighed. May as well tell her the truth. "This is my first time, too. I guess I lost control."

She burst into tears. "I'm not woman enough. Oh, Tom, I'm sorry."

Taking her into his arms, he rocked to soothe her. "You're plenty woman enough, my love, more than I was ready for. I know this is because of what Mary said. Don't let her get to you. She's nothing to me. I guess I'm inexperienced, too. We'll learn together."

Pulling back with an impish smile, she wiped her eyes. "Tom? I'm glad it was your first time."

He chuckled. "You know something? I'm glad it was your first time, too." He smoothed her hair from her face and kissed her nose. "You're bleeding. You can use the bathroom to clean up."

Blushing, she padded there and shut the door behind her.

Tom sat there, cursing himself. *I wanted her first time to be special. Something she would never forget. I have to admit I wasn't ready for such an intense sensation.* Discarding the rubber in the trash can, he wiped himself off with a tissue. *Damn.* He noticed the spots of blood on the sheet and made a mental note to change the bed himself.

****

Pam washed herself and glanced in the bathroom mirror. *What have I done? I swore I'd wait until I was married to do this. Am I really that weak? Or did Mary scare me into thinking I'd lose Tom?* Moving back, she felt a twinge where she was still sore. She had cleaned up the blood as best she could with the bathroom tissue. *Well, I have a pain to remind me for a time.*

She found Tom sitting on the bed with his

elbows on his knees and his face in his hands. He raised his eyes to her. "I'm truly sorry, Pam. I wanted this to be a wonderful memory, and I botched it."

Sitting beside him, she put her arms around him. "I know you love me, and that makes it wonderful."

Leaning in for a kiss, she noticed he was getting aroused. "Shall we try it again?"

Tom was speechless for a moment. "Aren't you too sore?"

Burying her face on his neck, she stirred his hair with her breath. "I can bear it."

Tom went to the dresser and returned with another packet while Pam lay back on the bed and drew Tom over to her. He was slow and they both were a little hesitant, but they soon discovered what pleased them. Gently, he led her to her first orgasm which took her on a flight of ecstasy. Afterward, they lay for a time in each other's arms.

Tenderly kissing her sweaty forehead, he ventured, "We'd better get dressed. MacGowen will be here in twenty minutes." She got up, collected her clothes, and headed toward the bathroom.

When she came out, Tom hobbled into the bathroom in his underwear. She went to the table and poured herself a bit more champagne and rolled it around on her tongue.

Tom, finished in the bathroom, saw her sitting at the table and sat across from her to take her hand. "Pam, I realize things have now changed, but one thing that hasn't changed is how I feel about you. You're still the most enchanting gi— *woman* I know."

"I guess I'm thinking that, now you're going to Tacoma, there will be more than just nurses. There will be female personnel and civilians—"

"Stop that!" He gave her hand a squeeze. "Yes,

I'm going to be around other women, but you will be the one I'll be thinking about. Don't sell yourself short. You're worth it."

Rising, she came around the table for a resounding kiss that warmed her doubts away. "I love you so much, I don't want to lose you to someone else."

"You won't," he said with a firm voice.

While they chatted away, Pam's fears were put into a far corner of her mind, and then she heard a knock at the door. Tom got up and opened it.

"Is Miss Wright ready to go back to the hotel, sir?" MacGowen asked.

Pam searched the lieutenant's face. *I wonder if there's any way he could tell what we were doing?* Was she wearing a neon sign saying, "She had sex!"?

Tom slipped on his jacket. "Yes. I'll ride with you." MacGowen helped Tom into the front, and Pam sat behind him with her arms draped around his shoulders. When they arrived, Pam hopped out and stood on the side of the jeep next to Tom.

"I'll see you at the docks tomorrow morning." The swell of love for him overcame her for a moment and tears blurred her vision. Touching her face, he kissed her goodnight. As the red sun swam on the horizon, she went through the doors of the lobby and turned back to watch the jeep pull away. She wasn't the same girl who had left the hotel this morning. *Tom and I will be all right. I can feel it in my bones.*

Pam opened the door to their room and found Addy sitting by the window, engrossed with the crossword puzzle in the newspaper. "How was your date, dear?" Studying Pam's face, Addy pursed her lips together, looked resigned, then smiled.

Pam suspected Addy knew what happened, and her cheeks heated up with shame. "We—worked out a lot of things."

Addy nodded. "I'm not going to pry or judge.

Lord knows, I've been there before. Just be fully aware of what you do." She yawned. "Well, I'm ready for bed." Drawing the curtains and turning down the sheets on the twin bed she'd chosen, Addy climbed in. "Goodnight, Pam."

Pam took her nightclothes into the bathroom and stopped at the door, glancing back. "Goodnight, Mrs. Shafer." Staring at her face in the bathroom mirror, she sighed. *Why do I always doubt Tom really loves me? He only had that one slip, but he didn't go through with it. I do believe him.* She rested her head against the cool glass. *I love him.*

Tom appeared the next morning while Addy and Pam were having breakfast at the hotel. "I thought I'd meet you here, instead. MacGowen loaded your cases into the jeep, and he'll drive us to the docks." He looked at Pam with a tender light in his eyes and clasped her hand in his. "I trust you slept well?"

Hesitating a moment, Pam smiled. "Yes, I did. You?"

Addy watched this exchange with an amused glint. "We have enough sugar on the table, thank you." She rose to leave. "Come on, you two. Pam and I have a ship to catch."

The women rode in the back of the jeep, bouncing over the gravel drive to the docks, the wind whipping their hats almost off their heads. The blue-and-white liner moored by the pier strained on its lashings as if it were eager to get going. MacGowen drove the jeep as close to the gangway as he could, helped Tom out, then offered to take the luggage to the check-in while they said their goodbyes.

Addy drew Tom away from Pam out of earshot and said something to him. Pam respected their privacy, but was curious. She looked questioningly at Tom as he came back to her when Addy started up the ramp.

Gripping both Pam's hands, he put several

kisses on the knuckles. "I love you so much. I ache every time we have to part."

She gently released her hands and fell into his warm embrace with the tears already coursing down her cheeks. "I wish this war to be over soon. At least they won't be shooting at you at the training grounds."

"I suspect Mom knows what we did last night, but I don't care." He kissed the tears off her face and gave her a kiss on the mouth that she felt all over. Even the champagne last night hadn't made her this lightheaded. She swayed at the knees as they pulled back. "Write to me in Tacoma."

"You know I will." After a gentle caress of his cheek, Pam headed for the ramp to join Addy on deck, where they leaned against the railing as the dockhands readied the liner to go.

She couldn't take her eyes off Tom. An invisible cord seemed to be attached between them. *It seems like a piece of myself will always be with him. He's a part of me now.*

As the tug guided the liner out to sea, Tom called out, "I love you!"

Pam blew him a kiss. "I love you, too!" She watched until she couldn't see him anymore, and then Addy put her arm around Pam's shoulder as the salty air stung their faces. They turned and went inside the observation room at the front of the ship to wait for the two-day trip to go by.

Addy brought over two frosty glasses of Coca-Cola and set them on the table between them. "Pam, if you were wondering what I said to Tom before we left, it was the same thing I said to you last night. You're both adults now and have to make your own decisions." She sighed after the last sentence, but it didn't look like she was angry with them, just resigned.

Taking a sip through the straw of the bubbly

liquid, Pam was thoughtful. "Thank you for being so understanding. I don't know if my father would take it so well."

Addy smiled. "Fathers are a little overprotective of their daughters. They tend to forget what they were like when courting."

The two women watched the glacial coastline as they headed home.

Chapter 13

Dear Son,
Well, the opening night went off without a hitch
and we seem to have a hit! Uncle Josh and I decided
to come on home because I, for one, have had enough
of New York. Em and Dave are quite the "toast of the
town." They're staying in the starring roles for a
while.

We'll come to Tacoma to see you before we catch
the flight to Juneau. We stopped in Evanston,
Indiana, to see our mother and family. I know you've
never met them because of our father, who just
passed on. We'll talk when we arrive.
Dad

Tom found things a little more relaxed at
McChord Field, being able to take time off without
miles of red tape. When he arrived at McChord, the
number of planes was staggering. They had
everything from the P-38 Lightnings to the B-24
Flying Fortresses, and now that his knee was more
flexible—he no longer required two canes to get
around, just one—he had been able to try the planes
out, to his delight, and had become an expert on
every craft there.

Standing at the Seattle depot waiting for the
Empire Builder to come in from out east, Tom dearly
wanted to go with his dad and his uncle to Juneau to
visit the family and Pam. Here it was December, and
it looked like he wouldn't get away until June. *The*
minute this war is over, I'm not going anywhere
without Pam. Her letters were filled with love and
longing.

Suddenly, Tom heard a whistle blow, and he glanced at the board. The train had arrived.

As he opened the door to the tracks, the December wind whipped around him and a heavy cold mist froze his face. He pulled his jacket tighter, and the smell of diesel fuel burned his nose. From beneath the bill of his hat he scanned the passengers coming off the train. Two familiar forms came toward him, and despite the cold stiffening his knee he hurried toward them, his cane making a muffled tap on the concrete walkway.

"Dad!" he shouted. "Uncle Josh!" They met in a three-way hug. "I have the jeep to take you to the airfield. How long do you have before your flight?"

Uncle Josh looked at his watch. "We've got three hours. I could do with some lunch. Where's the jeep?"

Gripping Tom's shoulder, his dad pointed. "Your leg's well enough to drive?"

Gee, I wish people would quit asking me about my knee. "It's stiff today, but I've been driving for a month or so. We've got the cover on the jeep, so you'll be out of the wind." Tom reached to take one of the suitcases, but his father stopped him.

"We can carry them. You lead the way."

The dark olive-green vehicle waited for them under a shelter in the parking lot. Uncle Josh climbed into the back with the luggage, and Tom and his dad sat in front. The wind had died down and mist hung thick and gray, so that Tom was glad he knew this way by heart. Finally, he saw the searchlight cutting through the fog and found the spot to park the jeep. After they stopped at the counter in the airport to check in the bags, the happy group headed to the small café.

When they'd given their order, Tom grinned at them. "I'm glad your show was such a hit in New York. I wish I could have seen it."

His dad nodded. "I wish the whole family had been there, but it was a thrill, believe me. I hated to leave Em there, but I have to remember she's an adult now."

Uncle Josh agreed. "We've been away from the family for six months. That's enough, in my book."

Tom looked up. "You know that Scott and Don enlisted last month, don't you? The last I heard from Mom was that they will be leaving after Christmas."

Uncle Josh sighed. "I was hoping the war would be over before your kid brother and my youngest son got into it."

Dad agreed. "It will be hard without the boys at the theater, and more for their mothers to worry about."

"And their fathers." Uncle Josh stared into his water glass as their order came.

After the waitress left, Tom was hesitant but nevertheless broached what might be a sensitive subject. "Dad, you told me in your letter you two stopped in Indiana to see your family. I know you told me quite a while ago that your father disowned both of you. So how did your mother find you?"

Putting down his sandwich and wiping his hands on his paper napkin, Dad began, "Before we left New York, we received a call from our sister, Ruth. She'd heard about us from the news of our show and finally got through to us to tell of our father's passing and that Mother would love to see us."

Uncle Josh took up the story. "We hadn't seen anyone from the family for more than twenty years and almost didn't recognize anyone. Mother isn't well, and she wanted to see all her children before she dies." He stopped for a moment as his voice broke at the end of the sentence. "We showed her the pictures we had with us and told her all about the family."

Dad put his hand on Josh's shoulder. "Mother said she was sorry our father drove all of us away. It wasn't until after the old man died that she first saw pictures of her grandchildren, even some that lived not far away." Dad glanced at Tom. "She said to tell you she was proud of you."

Staring at his plate, Tom put his fork down. "I'm glad you and Uncle Josh weren't like him."

"That's why we left the discipline to your mother and to your aunt. We didn't know if something would snap in us, because of our father, and we loved you kids too much to let that happen."

Their conversation went on to other things, and when the meal was finished, they went to the gate to wait for their flight. The wind had picked up again, lifting the fog, so as soon as the plane was ready they said their goodbyes. Dad gripped Tom's shoulders. "Will you be home for Christmas?"

Shaking his head, Tom was sad. "No, but I'll send presents up. My next leave will be in June." He watched his dad and uncle go up the steps to the plane.

I almost feel sorry for my grandfather. How can you treat anyone you love like that? He climbed into the jeep and drove back to the base, accompanied by the sun hanging over Puget Sound. Along the way he sent up a prayer for his grandfather's soul.

****

Dear Tom,

Yes, I do understand why you had to write to me for my permission. I'm happy to hear that the missions in Europe and the Pacific are going so well for the Allies now. I pray your younger brother and cousin won't see much action in France. Ted is sixteen now, and I worry that this war won't be over before he enlists.

Tom, of course you have my blessing to marry Pam. I'll be proud to have you for a son-in-law. You have seemed part of the family for many years. After you propose, we want to invite you and your family to a celebration in our backyard.

After the war is over, you may have your job back, if you want it. The option is open unless there is something else you want to do.

See you in June.

Bill Wright

****

Pam kicked around her bedroom, getting ready for work. *That damned army! I haven't seen Tom for a year, and they want to keep him another month. He deserves two weeks off after what he's been through.* It made her heady to think of last June in Anchorage, and Tom had written her faithfully every week since then. In his last letter, he'd told her of a special mission that might keep him away a while longer. *That damned army!*

Hurrying downstairs, she met her mother coming up. "Pam, dear, remember we're having a cookout for the neighbors Sunday. Remind the Shafers it will start at six o'clock." She put her hand on Pam's arm. "I know you're disappointed that Tom couldn't be here, but I'm sure you'll see him as soon as he can get away."

Pam nodded. "You're right. This isn't his fault." She kissed her mother's cheek. "I'll see you after work." She climbed into the car next to her father, and they headed toward the theater in relative silence until he pulled up in front of the lobby doors.

"See you later, princess." Squeezing her hand, there was a slight sadness in his eyes.

He hadn't called her "princess" for some time now. "Is something wrong, Dad?"

Smiling, he shook his head. "No. It's just you've grown up so fast, I have to stop myself sometimes to remember you're a young woman now, and not my little girl."

A great tenderness overwhelmed her. "No matter what, I'll always be your little girl." Part of her wondered what was going on with her parents. They both acted like she was dying or something. "Bye, Dad." She fled the car and ran into Ivan as she breezed through the lobby doors. "Oh, excuse me, Mr. Nikolaevich."

The big Russian bear of a man grinned. "No harm done, Miss Wright. By the way, Mr. Shafer wants to see you in his office. Something important, eh?" Then he chuckled and disappeared into the projection booth.

Pam stared after him. "Which Mr. Shafer?" But Ivan had already shut the door. *Well, I guess I'll find out.* Rapping on the office door, she ventured, "It's Pam. You wanted to see me?"

A muffled answer came from inside, and she turned the knob, then rapped on the door again. "Mr. Shafer?" Stepping into the office, she saw the form in the desk chair had his back to her and was leaning down, as if retrieving something off the floor. She stepped around the desk and was about to put her hand on his shoulder, saying, "May I—?" and then she screamed, "Tom!"

Flying backward into the file cabinets, she held her throat while her breath came in sputtering gasps. "What—? Where—? How—?" She swallowed a couple of times. "You seem to enjoy scaring me to death!"

Tom jumped out of the chair and came to her rescue. "You make it so much fun to do." Gathering her up in his arms, he looked her over. "Are you hurt?" At the shake of her head, he gave her a kiss that made her whole body squishy. She'd forgive him anything. Even sudden death. He hustled her over to the desk chair. "Sit!" he commanded, pushing her down by her shoulders and then settling back to lean against the desk.

"What are you doing?"

He put his fingers on her lips. "Shh, darling. Let me talk. My first day of school, I noticed a girl with golden pigtails sitting in front of me. I promptly pulled one of them. Do you know why?"

"I thought, at the time, you did it to annoy me. I remember you pestered me all through grammar school. I wished then you would go away and leave me alone." She sniffed at the memory.

"I didn't realize it at the time, but I wanted you to notice me. Anyway, do you remember the valentine I gave you when you were thirteen?"

Pam smiled. "That was the sweetest thing you had done up to then. I still have it tucked away in my trunk."

"Then there was our first formal dance in high school. You looked radiant in that pink satin gown, with your hair in that curly style around your shoulders. I felt like I was looking at a princess."

"You were very handsome in your dress suit." Pam was puzzled. "Why this trip down memory lane?"

The look on Tom's face turned very tender. "Because throughout most of my life, you've played a big part. As this war has gone on, you've been my anchor point. Remember the understanding talk we had at Jenny's wedding?" She nodded. "I didn't want to make you a young widow. I didn't know then how this war would go. Now, it looks like it will be over soon, and I'm not in real danger anymore." He ran his hands down her arms and took her hands in his. "Pam, I can't see a future for myself that you aren't in. I can't easily kneel, so I'm asking this way. Will you marry me when this war is over?"

A wave of emotion took her in its grasp, and she squeezed his hands tightly. This is what she'd been waiting for, for a long time, but now that it was said she was too overwhelmed to respond. Swallowing several times, she finally choked out, "I can't visualize my life without you. Yes."

Drawing her up, Tom took her in his arms and kissed her thoroughly. "I love you so much."

She cupped his face with both hands and gazed deep into his eyes with a promise of a lifetime of happiness shining there. "I love you, too."

He put his arm around her and guided her to the door. "Let's announce our engagement to the family." When they entered the restaurant, his whole family, minus the servicemen and Em, were there waiting.

Pam glanced at Tom. "Something tells me this wasn't a surprise to them."

He shrugged. "Well, I had to set it up."

Addy, standing by a table with Zeke, who was holding a champagne bottle, tapped her foot. "Well?"

Pam relished the suspense. Finally, she grinned. "I said yes."

Zeke popped the cork. "Congratulations to both of you!"

Jenny ran to hug Pam. "Now you'll truly be part of the family."

Pam made an announcement. "Remember, my family has a cookout in our backyard Sunday. Now we have something to tell them."

Tom cleared his throat. "They already know. That's what the party is about."

Pam put her fists on her hips. "They knew, too?"

Raising his glass to her, he grinned. "Of course. I had to ask your father's permission."

She gave a long-suffering sigh. "It's a good thing I said yes."

Everyone raised their glasses to the young couple and wished them the best in a future that looked considerably brighter.

After the day's celebration wound down, it was time to get the theater and restaurant ready for the night's business, with Tom helping Pam at the bar. He seemed to make sure he brushed behind her often with a "You smell terrific" or a grasp at the sides of her waist that made rippling waves go through her. Even when their sleeves slid against each other Pam was sure electric sparks were flashing between them. It was as if they had nothing on at all, and she was having trouble remembering recipes for the mixed drinks.

Cleaning a few of the glasses, she put them on the shelf while Tom arranged the new bottles of liquor he'd brought in from the cooler in the kitchen. She started talking to distract him and herself. "Is the war really about to be finished in Europe? Muriel told me she heard from Don that they were getting ready to march into Germany."

Tom nodded. "I heard that, too. The Germans had a tough time with the Russians, and they couldn't keep up with the Americans and English hitting them on the western front at the same time. I'm just happy both Scott and Don survived D-Day. Don't tell Mom or Auntie, but that was a suicide mission."

An order came in for four beers, and Tom took them to the table while Pam made some mixed drinks at the bar. When the movie started, most of the restaurant patrons retired to the theater, but Tom and Pam sat at one of the small tables with Jenny.

Putting his hand over Jenny's, Tom said with compassion, "How are you doing, kid?"

She gave him a small smile. "Glad to be busy, so I don't have to think so much. I miss Chase terribly, but I have to go on, for Junior. I worry a lot of the time about all of you in service."

About an hour before closing time, Pam called her father and told him Tom was bringing her home. "Dad, he and I have some things to discuss. I'll see you later."

"Take as much time as you need. And congratulations to you both."

"Thanks, Dad." Hanging up, she said her goodnights to the Shafers while Tom waited for her in the station wagon. Zeke and Addy were going home in Josh's Hudson.

Tom drove down to the abandoned area where the Treadwell gold mines used to be. Not many clues were left that mining had been a thriving industry here, fifty years before. Now it was a wild area by the channel, with the wind whipping through the foundations of a company town. With the closing of the Alaska-Juneau mine this year, an era had slipped away.

It was a well-known parking spot, and they had often come here, as many high schoolers did, to talk and pet, although not as much during the summer, because of the long, sunlit days here in Alaska. Tom stopped the car on a ridge overlooking the channel, and they sat down on the long grass next to the rocks and watched as the seabirds flitted, diving in the sparkling waters. The salty smell of the ocean was on the breeze caressing Pam's face.

Interlacing his fingers through hers, Tom said, "We should talk about what we want after we're married. In your father's letter back to me, he offered my old job back when the war ends, but I haven't decided what I really want to do with my life yet."

Pam put her head on his shoulder. "I'd like to stay here in Juneau, since we both have our families here."

He nodded. "I'd want that, too, but what if we have to move for some reason? We've just come out of a depression. Who knows if it's going to happen again?"

She thought about all the hardships her family

had gone through in the thirties. "We can face anything together. Your family had to keep moving from where they were born, so if we have to, we can, too." She felt her cheeks glow. "What about children?"

Tom laughed. "A dozen, at least. No, we'll take care of what we have." He gazed at her with heated eyes. "That'll be the best job of all."

Running her fingers up the back of his neck, she drew him into a kiss that deepened as he ran his hand over her breast. She felt the nipple tighten to greet him, being swept up in a wave of desire while every part of her body reached for this man who loved her.

Taking a quick look around, Tom said in a husky voice, "No one is here..." Reaching into his pocket, he drew out a small packet.

A moral shock went through her system, and she gave an erotic jerk. "Out here in the open?"

"Why not?" he said, and his lips claimed hers again as they lay back into the tall grass. "We can do this, with a little rearranging of clothes." Unbuttoning her blouse, he freed a breast from her bra and the nipple immediately puckered in the cool air. "Beautiful," he said between gasps.

Heat went through her as he sucked the tip, and she felt a hard hot bulge on her thigh. "Your turn," she said as she opened his belt and trousers, moving them down his hips. He hissed as she gently stroked his shaft.

They both spent time finding places that responded to a caress, a kiss, or a nip. Pam's whole body seemed to be vibrating to the electricity of his touch.

As he removed the rubber from its packet, she shed her already soaked panties, and he moved on top of her. She could feel him at the entrance of her body, where he stroked her once with his fingers, then thrust in and—no pain, only pleasure.

Building, building as he moved in and out, Pam felt as one with the universe. The grass kept up a rhythmic crunching underneath them as she soared as high as the seabirds on waves of ecstasy. Tom kissed her before she shattered into pieces and took him with her. The ripples finally calmed and she came to reality in his arms. "I love you."

Brushing his hand through her hair, he whispered in her ear, "I love you, too." He rolled off her and they held each other in an embrace in their enchanted wonderland by the water. After a while, he checked his watch. "We should be going." Straightening up their clothing, they went to the car, where he gazed at her as he started the engine. "Getting back to you is what I'm fighting for."

Pam stretched her legs as they drove home. *I'm so lucky to have Tom. Please, Lord, keep him safe and let him return to me.*

Sitting in front of her house, Tom caressed her cheek. "I can't wait until we don't have to part anymore. I want to take you home with me."

Her eyes misted. "I want that, too." They leaned toward each other for a last passionate kiss. As Pam pulled back, she smiled. "Look." She pointed to the porch.

Tom looked puzzled. "What? There's no one out there."

"Yes."

Dawn came to his face. "Oh." Then he kissed her again. "Let me help you get rid of some evidence." He gently pulled a couple of long grass blades from her hair.

"I'll bet I have green stains on the back of my skirt," Pam said, as he helped her out of the car.

Tom turned her around. "Not bad. You could say we were sitting at the seaside—which we were." Grabbing her by the waist, he whirled her around at the base of the steps, and she put her arms around his neck and kissed him full on the lips.

Tom set her down on wobbly legs. "I'll find a ring for you as soon as I can."

"We can go together to the jewelry store sometime this week and pick our rings out."

"Good idea. That's one thing we can take care of soon. Until tomorrow, goodnight, my love."

Standing locked in an embrace for a few more minutes, Pam didn't want to let go, but then Tom took her hands and kissed her fingers. She leaned on the porch railing until the station wagon was out of sight.

Chapter 14

My love,
Here it is October and it doesn't look like you'll be home for Christmas again. The Germans and Japanese don't seem to realize that they've been defeated. This war is going to stretch on until the last person is left standing in both countries.

Here's a new picture of me to carry with you. You notice the lovely ring is visible. I'm so in love with you, I can't think of anything else. I've been working on household things, so we'll be ready to settle down when you get back.

If you ever get lonely, just think of our summer enchantment by the sea.

Love always,
Pam

The McChord loudspeaker blared out with a list of five names to come to Colonel Washington's office. Tom's name was one of them. *Now, what did I do to be called into the commander's inner sanctum?* Tom left his class studying the B-24's schematics and headed to administration.

A few minutes later, he was standing at attention with four other pilots in front of McChord's chief. The colonel signaled for them to be at ease.

"Men, I'll come right to the point. You have been chosen for a mission. All of you are experts in the B-29 Superfortress and are needed on a mission which, we hope, will bring Japan to its knees. By November tenth, you should be assembled at Tinian in the Marianas, along with other expert pilots from all bases, to launch what will be called Operation

Downfall. It will be organized into the Twenty-First Bomber Command. You'll have a week to wrap up things here. Your crew will be chosen from the men at our base, and then you will fly to Tinian, where you will get your instructions. Any questions?"

Excitement charged through Tom. They were letting him back into combat, he was sure. "No questions, sir," came the reply from the five.

In the following days, Tom's elation mingled with a touch of fear that kept his adrenaline up, dashing off letters to Pam and his parents that the army had assigned him a new mission but he couldn't say what and where, just pray for his safe return. It was wonderful to feel needed again.

On the morning of the flight, the crews assembled on the tarmac. It was the culmination of intense special training for the mission: every pilot, engineer, bombardier, radioman, navigator, and gunner knew their position and equipment inside and out. The brand-new B-29s shone, even in the cold and mist of the November Puget Sound.

Major Stanford, the head of flight training, met them that morning. "Men, congratulations on being chosen for this very important mission, one which will be the end of the Empire of Japan. When you reach the base in the Marianas, you will receive further instructions. Good luck, men, and may God go with you." He saluted them all.

Tom climbed into the cockpit of his massive airplane. He had nicknamed it "Alaskan Angel" and painted it on the side with a blonde beauty in a form-fitting parka, sitting on a snowbank, her long legs bare and a small halo over her head. Tom wasn't going anywhere without Pam.

The first thing Tom and his co-pilot, Lieutenant Pete Cummings, did was fire up the engines, warming them up for the flight. Pete was a red-haired, freckle-faced kid from Nebraska who had been flying crop dusters from the time he was sixteen. Tom considered him one of his best students and was happy when his request for Pete to be his co-pilot was granted.

Their engineer, Lieutenant Frank Tatum, popped his head into the cockpit. "The crew is all assembled, sir," he said, saluting Tom.

"Thank you, Lieutenant." Tom picked up the intercom mike. "Gentlemen, in a few moments we'll be leaving for the first leg of our journey. Tonight we'll be at Hickum Field on Oahu. The trip will take three days to get to Tinian, over secured ocean. We will travel by day and stay overnight on the refueling stops. I want you to stay reasonably sober and be assembled on the tarmacs ready to go at oh-six hundred every morning. Understood?" At echoes of acknowledgments ringing around the large plane, he added, "At the signal from the tower, we're off. May God go with us."

A few minutes later, the five B-29s were up above the cold November clouds, heading for the warm tropic climes of Hawaii. The hum of the big engine props vibrated through the Superfortress, something Tom didn't mind, but he was glad these planes were pressurized. The discomfort of icy temperatures because of altitude was a thing of the past.

During the eight-hour flight, Tom and Pete took turns at the helm, and the sun was hovering near the horizon as they saw the welcome chain of islands poking out of the endless ocean. They sighted the field near Pearl Harbor and got permission to land the five aircraft. There were still a few damaged areas from the attack a few years ago, but Hickum Field was back in business. They taxied to where a number of B-29s were parked in the refueling docks, and the ground personnel directed them to where they were to park the plane.

After the crew was out, Tom took a walk through the interior to make sure everything was secure. Coming out of the hatch, he felt the warm island breeze that carried the scent of the sea and flowers. Tom had never been to Hawaii before, but he was sure he could get to like it.

The crew was talking to a sergeant at the wheel of a jeep when Tom came up, and the sergeant saluted. "Captain, I just told your crew that the guest quarters are in that building over there." He pointed to a large white dormitory structure. "You may spend the night there."

Tom returned his salute. "Thank you, Sergeant." He turned to the crew. "Men?" They started the walk to quarters. While the crew were being assigned their rooms, Tom heard a cheery greeting behind him, and when he turned there was his old wingman, Ken Edwards, coming toward him. The two beat each other on the back. "Damn, Ken, it's good to see you again! You're a captain now, too!"

"You're going to Tinian? They let a lame horse out on the range?"

Tom laughed. "Just have a bit of a limp. I can still fly a plane."

"Some time ago, I offered to meet you for dinner at the O-club, and you stood me up. Join me tonight and we can catch up."

"Where is it?"

Ken pointed out the window to a building across the road. "It's over there. I'll meet you here in the lobby in an hour."

The two went to their respective rooms to settle in, and after freshening up and putting on a change of clothes, Tom met Ken and they went to the busy O-club. There must have been thirty crews headed to Tinian, and the place was packed with overnighters.

Biting with relish into his hamburger, Tom dug in. Between that and his order of chips and Coca-

Cola, he asked, "Ken, did you come from Elmendorf in your B-29?"

Ken nodded. "Seems we've been chosen for a big mission against the Japs. That's all they would tell us."

"Same here. They said we'd get more orders when we reached Tinian. We have one more refueling overnight on Midway."

Ken grinned. "I hope they can get all our planes on that little speck of an island. We might be tighter than a cattle car going to market."

"What have you been up to since I last saw you?"

"It's been mighty quiet after the Japs hightailed it off the islands. We've been patrolling the Aleutians but haven't found anything. In fact, a lot of the forces have been stationed elsewhere. It was my turn, I guess."

They continued to exchange what they had been up to and faced since they last met. Tom told him about training new pilots and getting engaged.

"Congratulations! Is it to that sweet little filly I saw at the hospital?"

Tom smiled. "She gives me incentive to come back alive."

"I went back to Texas on a couple of leaves. Last time, my dad informed me that meat had been taken off rationing. Looks like everyone thinks this war will be over before long, which is fine with me."

The two captains visited for a few hours before they called it a night, with a light rain coming gently down as they hurried to their quarters. There would be time for more conversations in the days ahead.

****

My dearest,

The mission I'm on is going very well. Remember Ken Edwards, who used to be my wingman? You met him at the hospital. Anyway, we are working on the same mission at the same base. It's nice to have a

162

buddy back again.

Hope things are going well with all of you and especially my wife-to-be. Get things set up there, because I think it won't be much longer.

As always, pray for me, love.

Tom

Pam and Jenny were busy setting up the restaurant and bar for the night's movie crowd. The May days were getting longer, although not brighter, with the ever-present fog off the sea. This had been a drearier May than usual, but more people were coming to the movies.

Jenny's waitresses scurried around, setting the tables with fresh linen and silverware, and fresh flower centerpieces. They had hired another cook to give Amelia a hand on their busiest days. Now, with many items off the rations list, they had a full daily menu.

Suddenly, she heard shouts and screams coming from the office. Addy and Muriel hurried out the door and into the restaurant, with Pam feeling a twist in the bottom of her stomach. *Oh, my God, someone's dead.*

Addy hugged Pam, and Muriel grabbed Jenny as Addy sang out, "We heard on the radio that Germany surrendered today!" Everyone in the restaurant jumped up and down and yelled, bringing the men in from the theater.

Hearing the news, Josh went into the cooler in the kitchen and brought out a bottle of champagne. "That means Don and Scott will be coming home!"

Pam squeezed Addy's hand. "Any word on Japan?"

Addy shook her head. "Apparently, that side hasn't ended yet."

The news was bittersweet. It sounded like the war was finally going to be over, but the Japs were being stubborn. If only Tom could come home, too.

Almost another year had come and gone since she'd last seen him. She would be an old woman by the time she was able to marry, at this rate.

Jenny picked up Chase from the playpen in the office and came out with an envelope addressed to Pam. "I found this in today's mail that Mother just brought in from the post office. It looks like an APO from Europe."

Addy gave Pam a glass of champagne. "Who do you know in Europe?"

"Outside of Scott and Don, no one who would write to me."

Jenny poked her. "Open it."

Putting her finger under the sealed flap, she tore it. A single folded piece of paper was in there. Shaking it out, she saw one word on the sheet, "Soon." A chill went up her spine and she dropped the paper to the floor.

Addy retrieved it. "What does this mean?"

Pam shook her head. "I don't know. There's no name on this at all."

Addy and Jenny glanced at each other with worried faces, then Addy tossed the letter aside. "Come, let's celebrate. We can deal with this another time." They rejoined the group giving toasts to God and Country.

Chapter 15

My dearest love,
Since the Germans surrendered, I wait every day
for the news that the Japanese did, too. I heard about
the bombings over the cities there and I assume that's
where you are. Stay safe, Tom, I need you.
Things are going well here. The summer season
is at its peak and, I'm sure your parents told you,
Scott and Don came home from Europe banged up
and scarred, but at least alive. Jenny wouldn't stop
hugging them. Look at the greeting you, Hank, and
Joe will receive!
Tell the Japs to hurry up so we can be married
before Christmas. I love you so.
Pam

Tom opened the door to his Quonset hut and the
warm tropic breeze hit him. It had been brutally hot
for the last few days, and the breeze seemed to help.
He'd never known a time when the sea wind was
anything but chilly. Here, there were days when
there was no wind at all, and it was easy to
understand how much trouble that must have
caused sailors years ago. Perhaps the unlucky
gremlins that bedeviled the sailing ships were
tampering with the B-29s; several of them had
crashed at the end of the runway, their twisted
skeletons piled like a warning.

The few palms around the hut cast lacy shadows
that played along the ground. He took off his
uniform jacket and rolled his shirt sleeves up before
he left, with Ken catching up with him as they both
headed to the officers' mess.

Ken didn't look the worse for wear in this heat. "Now, this is more like a Texas day."

Glancing at him, Tom smiled. "I guess neither of us would last in the other's state, would we?"

"All in what you're used to, I guess."

In the line at breakfast, Tom declined the coffee and opted for a glass of water, instead, before sitting at a table with several of the other pilots.

Tom sighed. "Here it is the beginning of August, and the Japs still haven't surrendered. What do we have to do to them?"

Ken nodded. "You'd think burning their cities down would have brought them around. They're as crazy as if they were chewing on loco weed."

Another pilot added, "Well, we have mines all around the island now. Today, we're supposed to finish off the fleet."

After breakfast, everyone made their way to the tarmac to meet their crews and climb into the loaded planes. Tom and Pete switched on the engines, listening as the mighty plane rumbled to life. Frank poked his head in the door. "Crew's all assembled, sir."

Tom picked up the intercom mike. "Men, orders today are to take out the remaining fleet south of Japan. There shouldn't be much resistance, but be on the lookout for anything. God go with us." Setting his mouth in a tight line, he glanced at Pete.

Pete met his eyes. "Ready, sir."

They taxied to the runway and were in the air on course to Japan when the navigator called out the heading to where the enemy ships had been sighted. Tom had taken the point to the bomb site, then handed the controls to the bombardier, who centered on his targets. After dropping their load, they flew back. There was very little resistance from below.

Keeping his eyes over the water, Tom looked for the form of Tinian. "Hell of a war, eh, Lieutenant?"

Pete sat back, watching the gauges. "Yes, sir. I wonder how long it will take before the Japs holler uncle?"

"I think that's on everybody's mind right now. Anxious to get home?"

"Yes, sir. Got a farm to help take care of. Want to marry and settle down on my own acres and raise me some wheat. You, sir?"

"I've got my girl I'm engaged to." The warmth spread over him at the thought of his Alaskan Angel. "Don't know yet what I want to do after the war. Might go back to flying the mail plane again. Or an airliner." Tom smiled. "But who would want to come to Alaska?"

"You told me you get tourists in Juneau, sir."

"Because it's the territorial capitol. Outside of the panhandle, it's mostly ice and Eskimos."

The airstrip at Tinian came into view and, one by one, the B-29s glided into the base. Tom taxied toward the refueling area and parked the plane. As the crew tumbled out of the hatch, Tom and the engineer checked the interior before sliding out themselves.

The red sun was slipping toward the flat horizon. *At least the hot summer days aren't as long here as they are in Alaska.* Tom removed his cap and mopped the sweat off his forehead. Heading to the officers' mess, he ran into Ken. "Join me for dinner?"

"Sure. Chow sounds mighty good right now."

While they were enjoying a repast of army food, the loudspeaker crackled to life. "Will the following personnel report to the colonel's office at oh-nineteen hundred hours—" Both Ken and Tom were on that list.

Ken threw his biscuit on his plate. "Oh, hell, what did we do now?"

Tom glanced at Ken. "Looks like we'll find out in a half-hour. Hey, they have that pudding that can bounce off walls. Let's get some before we go to the office."

At oh-nineteen hours, Tom and Ken were standing at attention with four other pilots in Colonel Hammond's office. "Men, I called you in here about your mission tomorrow, per Commander Farrell's orders." He indicated a young colonel standing at the other side of his desk. "This is Colonel Tibbets of the 509th Composite Group. He'll explain the change of plans. Colonel?"

Tibbets nodded to the pilots. "Men, at ease and have a seat." He waved his hand toward the chairs behind them. When they again turned their attention to him, he continued, "We're on a top secret mission. I'm sure you've heard about the USS Indianapolis unloading equipment and crates here today. This is what will end this war. I can't reveal yet what we have, but I'm here to inform you that your bombing run is canceled." A murmur went through the pilots. "I'm going to take off tomorrow morning with my crew and head to Japan with two other planes from our base. What I have will devastate the enemy country."

A hand went up and, at the colonel's nod, the pilot asked, "Isn't that dangerous, to go alone into enemy territory, sir? I mean, their defenses are down, but they still have enough to take out one plane."

"We think that if they see just one plane, they might think it's a scouting mission and ignore it. Which is what we're hoping for. I'm sorry I can't tell you anything else. Tomorrow at this time, we'll be back, and then maybe we can all go home. Dismissed."

Tom, Ken and the other pilots decided to go over to the O-club, where Ken sat next to Tom at a small table. "What the hell does he have? He seems convinced he could wipe Japan off the map."

Tom shrugged. "Who knows what the government came up with this time, but if it means going home, I'm all for it."

A few of the 509th crew came into the club and ordered some beers. One of the pilots hollered out to them, "Hey, fellas! We were told you came to end the war. Where have you been? We could have used you years ago!" A spattering of laughter ran through the crowd.

One of the 509th called back, "Just you wait! You'll be kissing our asses tomorrow!"

Ken glanced at Tom and raised his beer bottle. "Here's to anything that gets us out of Hell."

Tom did likewise and took a swig of the amber liquid. *I hope I can cope with peacetime. It seems like I've been in the army all my life.* Sighing, he turned his attention back to the camaraderie of a bunch of war-weary pilots.

Twenty-four hours later, Tom and the other pilots were staring in shock at the pictures taken from the Enola Gay and from intelligence cameras stationed outside the bombed area. A huge column of smoke that looked like a mushroom filled the frame. Colonel Tibbets faced them all. "That's what we were carrying. It's an atomic bomb, designed and tested by a group of scientists known by a code name: the Manhattan Project. It seemed to take out the entire city of Hiroshima. We are waiting for word of Japan's surrender, or we may drop another one of these on them, for good measure."

Whistling under his breath, Ken leaned toward Tom. "Good God, what have weapons come to? If that's the new age, we could destroy each other in less than a week."

Awestruck, yet scared at the same time, Tom was stunned. With a weapon like this, the world would have to either maintain peace or face annihilation. He knew America wouldn't be able to hold onto its secret for long. What kind of existence would there be for anyone in the future?

Tom expressed his thoughts to Ken over a beer at the O-club. "I heard that intelligence said people were vaporized near ground zero and there were radiation burns on many farther out."

Ken nodded. "It's a good thing we got it first. I read that the Germans were playing around with heavy water, before the Norwegians sabotaged the plant."

"Heavy water?"

"Seems like that's something you need for an atomic bomb."

Tom shook his head. "Everyone thought the Great War would end all wars. Instead, it looks like the conflicts are just getting worse."

Ken lifted his bottle in a salute. "Here's to the scientists who come up with bigger and better ways for us to kill each other."

Tom clinked his bottle to Ken's. *I hope mankind will still be around in ten years' time.*

That night, Tom had nightmares about dropping one atomic bomb after another until the earth vaporized. He woke in a cold sweat.

****

Pam pounded on the table in frustration. "I can't believe Japan would hesitate to surrender after two of those horrible bombs were dropped on their cities. You'd think they'd give up just to save their people."

Shaking her head, Jenny said, "There have been so many false reports, it's hard to know what's true and what isn't."

"Everyone got so excited at that news story two days ago saying Japan had surrendered, and then a few minutes later it was, 'Nope, they didn't.'"

Glancing at her watch, Jenny remarked, "It's ten to three. May as well finish setting up for the movie crowd." She got up and disappeared into the kitchen, while Pam headed to the bar, where she set up the clean glasses and turned on the radio. Music would take her mind off things while she swayed her hips to "Take the A Train" and the glasses thunked down in a straight row.

Suddenly, the microphone crackled to life and the announcer came on. "Ladies and gentlemen, we have news coming in from Washington, D.C."

Pam quickly called everyone in, and they stared, breathless, at the radio. "Ladies and gentlemen, President Harry Truman has stated to the press that he received a message of surrender from the Japanese government..." The rest of the statement was lost in the roar of excitement in the room. Pam, caught up in the rolling sea of hugs and kisses all around, could easily have flown to the moon with her arms outstretched. The waitresses were in a massive hug and jumping up and down, while Addy and Zeke did an impromptu tango around the dance floor. Josh whirled Muriel off her feet as Ivan and Kata shouted out their joy. Jenny found Pam and Amelia, and the three cried on each other's shoulders while laughing out loud.

Hearing celebration from the streets, they all moved out into the lobby, where the two younger Shafer men, Don and Scott, were cheering, and Don had his nephew, Chase, on top of his shoulders while the toddler grinned and pulled Don's hair. Scott had the Nikoleavichs' daughter, Marita, in a close embrace—they had become quite an item since the boys came home from Europe.

Josh jabbed Zeke in the ribs and said something to him. The two men quickly disappeared into the kitchen and returned with a barrel they rolled out onto the street. Addy brought out two boxes of large Dixie cups as Josh waved and hollered, "Free beer for everyone!"

It seemed as though the whole city was out in

the streets, and Pam got caught up in the tidal wave of humanity as the undulating crowd took on a life of its own. The police and the sheriff's department were out in force, but they didn't try to control the jubilant throng.

Out in the harbor, the fireboats sprayed water high in the air, while liners and navy boats shot flares up in a vast display of color and light.

Several sailors headed toward Pam, and she was caught and kissed numerous times as she and some of the other girls were passed along the gauntlet of happy navy men.

A conga line of men, women, and children wound its way down the street, and a mother led her children in a thrown-together parade. The children had horns, drums, and cymbals that made a loud racket, while flag-waving people fell in behind them.

As the booze took hold, several people ran down the street barely dressed, a couple of them not at all. Some of the Christian community knelt on the sidewalk in prayer alongside the revelers, unbothered by the others, who cared not at all what anyone else did. Everyone had their own way of praising the end of the war, while confetti and toilet paper were thrown and covered everything.

Pam was in a kaleidoscope requiring all her senses—flares and fireworks filling the skies, the din of voices and noisemakers, smells of sulfur and beer, the surge of the mass of humanity, even the taste of the air and its freedom from worry over the safety of loved ones.

Later, she found her way back to the front of the theater, where Josh had his banjo and was leading a joyous throng in "Happy Days Are Here Again." No one was inside, although it was past time for the movie; the entire afternoon was filled with celebration. Pam sank to her knees in the aisle, her hands reaching to the ceiling. "Praise God it's over.

Now bring my Tom safely home," she cried, her tears making rivulets down her cheeks. Then she buried her face in her hands as huge sobs wracked her body.

Chapter 16

Tom paused a moment while packing his duffel bag for the trip home. The papers were in front of him for his three-month furlough to decide whether he wanted to make the army his career. He had obtained the rank of major, but he was still unsure what he wanted to do. Talking it over with Pam seemed the right thing to do since it would involve her future, as well. It could mean being away from her for months at a time.

He picked up her picture, the one he always carried with him, and that familiar velvety feeling came over him. Of all he missed of home, she was the top. It was Pam who kept him going, his light at the end of this horrible tunnel. He'd told her to begin on the wedding plans, and she had written that Kata was starting her gown.

His co-pilot, Pete Cummings, came into the room they'd shared with the bombardier and navigator, who had already left that morning. "Sir, I came to say goodbye and it was an honor to serve with you."

Smiling at the young man, Tom nodded. "I'm happy they assigned you to me. I knew you were the best pilot in my classes." He shook Pete's hand. "I wasn't wrong."

"Sir, are you leaving on the transport to Honolulu in an hour?"

"Yes, are you going on the same one? That's the one that heads back to Seattle."

"No, sir, I'm leaving tomorrow to catch the flight for San Francisco. I wish you well in the future. I know you said you didn't know what you wanted to do."

Tom grinned. "I'll make my mind up. Good luck on getting your farm started."

"Yes, sir."

Slapping Pete on the shoulder, Tom swung the duffel over his arm. "Goodbye, Pete."

The tarmac gave off waves of heat in the relentless tropical sun, and Tom grinned, happy to be going back to a cooler part of the world. Just then his eye caught a figure leaning against the chain-link fence—Ken Edwards, who waved and started his way.

Tom dropped his bag to the ground as Ken clamped a hand on his shoulder and wordlessly gazed at him. The two hugged like long-lost brothers until Ken pulled back, quickly dashing the tears in his eyes. "It's hard to say goodbye to you, buddy. I guess the distance of our two homes is too great to have a gab at the watering hole."

Tom equally choked up. "I'll never forget the dusty old cowboy who saved my skin. I can't thank you enough for that. Are you staying in the army?"

"Nah, too damn tired of the military. I'm going back to ranching. Maybe get me my own spread. You going back to flying the mail?"

"Don't know yet." The plane started warming up, and Tom picked up his bag. "Got to go. Goodbye, Cowboy."

Ken waved as Tom boarded the transport. "Adios, Buck."

It was a long trip, stopping at Honolulu, then picking up the transport to Seattle. On the final leg, from Seattle to the airfield in Juneau, Tom watched through the window of the transport for the familiar mountains of home.

The Gastineau Channel came into view, and soon Mount Juneau was in his line of sight. Home.

The plane circled and headed to the airfield outside of town, carrying a number of war-weary soldiers and sailors on this trip from Honolulu. They were on their way back to their lives, no longer the fresh-faced kids who had left with glory in their hearts. Tom felt forty years older.

He rubbed his eyes as the plane taxied into the disembarking area, where a crowd of welcomers stood by the gate outside the tarmac. As the stairs were rolled to the door hatch, the passengers lined up in the aisle. Tom hoisted his duffel bag to his shoulder and, one by one, the servicemen traveled down the steps to a joyous reception with family and friends.

His eyes misted when he caught sight of Pam in the midst of his family, sophisticated in a lavender suit with a snowy blouse and wrist-length gloves. A matching veiled hat was perched on her short curly hair. She was no longer the girl he once knew. In her place stood a world-wise woman, and that was what he needed. He set his duffel bag beside him.

First to greet him were his parents. His father slapped him on the back, and his mother buried her face on his chest and cried. Scott was there, looking every inch a man. After he'd hugged his brother, everyone stood back and let the young couple find each other.

Fitting into his arms, Pam kissed him, and he found his heaven in her, with her perfume surrounding his senses, and he knew he truly was home. How healing was a good woman, and he was growing hard when they broke their kiss. Here would not be a good time.

They all piled into the station wagon, and Tom decided then and there he would call it quits with the army. There were so many other choices that would include Pam.

At the theater, he greeted the rest of the family.

Outside of Emily, everyone was there; apparently he was the last one discharged. Hank and Joe, in civilian clothes, banged him around, and then Jenny grabbed him and gave a super hug, praising God the whole time. Tom picked up Chase and swung him up in the air, while the toddler giggled. What did men do who had no family?

Since it was Monday, the theater and restaurant were closed, so the family retired to the dining area, along with the Nikolaevichs, who would soon be even more a part of the family than they'd been already, Tom judged, watching Scott and Marita. Amelia and Muriel had been busy setting the tables together into one long assembly and loading it with a feast.

Josh came out with a case of champagne. "We've been saving this for the war's end and we had all our military home. Now, with Tom, everyone is home, a little battered but alive." Popping the cork on one bottle, he started filling glasses. "Before we toast to the heroes, let's have a moment of silence for the ones like Chase, who paid the ultimate price." Muriel put her arm around Jenny, and Josh glanced around the table. "Hank, Tom, Joe, Scott, and Don, thank you for putting your lives on the line for your country. And thanks to the rest of you for keeping things running smoothly here. To me, you are all heroes." He lifted his glass to the room. "God bless this family and friends!"

They stood and toasted each other, and Tom and Pam each took a sip, smiling. Then everyone sat and dug into the honey-jeweled ham, roasted potatoes, candied carrots, rolls, and relishes, a meal topped off with summer-berry pie and ice cream.

Tom elbowed Hank, who was seated on the other side of him. "What happened to Patsy?"

He shrugged. "We were just too different. It didn't last."

"Sorry. I didn't know."

"I can take it. Now, I'm open to any pretty face." He gave his signature grin, and Tom laughed. "So when are you two getting hitched?"

Pam leaned to speak to Hank. "We have to talk to my parents sometime this week."

Kissing her cheek, Tom warmed. "This stint is far more preferable to the last one."

With mock anger on her face, Pam remarked, "You mean talking to my parents is like fighting a war?"

Hank chuckled. "Now, you've put your foot in it, soldier boy."

Dinner ended on a high note, with everyone relaxed and happy without the war hanging over them. Zeke hauled out the turntable and records, and they all danced, just like old times.

While Tom held Pam and swayed to "Always," it seemed as though the war didn't happen and it all was a bad dream, but the twinge in his knee soon let him know different. "Let's sit this one out," he whispered in her ear. As they sat at the table, Tom took her hand. "My knee still bothers me at times."

"Is it bad?" she asked with a concerned look.

He kissed her fingers. "Every once in a while. I need a cane if I have to do a lot of walking. It gets weak, not sore."

Hank popped over to the table. "Hey, Tom, can I borrow Pam for a jitterbug?"

Tom glanced at Pam. "Up to you."

Her face lit up. "You're on, hep-cat!" They swung onto the floor, truckin' to "In the Mood."

Tom ground his teeth. He used to cut a mean rug, and Pam moved to the music like she was born to dance. He watched with envy and a touch of jealousy as Hank put his hands on her waist and lifted her high to the beat.

When the number ended, they breathlessly hugged and laughed before Pam kissed Hank's cheek and made her way back to Tom, who gave her an unfocused stare. "Say, Miss Bartender, could you make me a whiskey, straight up?"

Pam bit her lip. "Isn't that a little strong after champagne and beer?"

"Just do it. I need it after the four years I've been through."

Pam shrugged. "Well, it *is* your first night as a civilian, but don't let this become a habit."

Hitting his fist against the table, he hissed, "For once, don't act like a mother hen!"

Pam and everyone within earshot looked shocked, and Pam hurried to the bar, coming back with the whiskey. "Here, but I'm going to find someone else who can take me home."

Hank came up behind her. "Pam, I'll drive you."

Tom stood, swaying a bit. "My good ole cousin, taking home my girl."

Hank patted his shoulder. "Just trying to keep her safe for you. Come on, Pam, I'll get your sweater."

Giving Tom a quick kiss, she whispered, "I'll talk to you in the morning. Goodnight." She followed Hank out.

Dad pulled up a chair across from Tom. "You've been hitting the booze pretty hard tonight. What's wrong?"

Taking another swig, Tom hiccuped. "Lost four years of my life, Dad. Knee still gets weak once in a while, and it's been two years since I was shot. I've decided not to go back into the army, but I don't know what I want to do." He looked into his father's eyes. "Does that make sense to you?"

"You and the others just got back from a trip to hell. I can't even guess what it's like, but I do know you won't find any answers in that stuff." He pointed to the glass. "Don't come home and crawl into a bottle. You'll lose everything important to you, and that won't be fair to Pam. You won't find a girl that loves you more."

Anger surged through him. "You've never been in a war. You don't know what it's like to be in danger all the time."

His dad shook his head. "Now that, I probably realize more than you think. Especially if you get on the wrong side of a crime family." He glanced at Tom and sighed. "I never went into detail about why your mother and I came up here to Juneau, but it wasn't just to help Josh. We were both almost killed for exposing the distillery that was set up at the studio we worked for. They found us up here and almost got us, but they were caught by the authorities. They're still in prison, as far as I know."

Tom wasn't impressed. "I didn't have someone else mopping up for me. I had to do it myself. Not good enough, Dad."

His dad stood. "Come on, son, the party's breaking up. Let's go home, and you can sleep it off and start fresh tomorrow."

Tom took another swig from his glass, then stood, unsteady. His father gave him a hand, and they headed for the cars.

At home, after finding his way upstairs to his room, he slipped off his shoes and lay back on top of the bedspread. Home. Or was it? Gracing the bookshelves were the model airplanes that the child he was had worked on so long ago. A high school banner spread over his chest of drawers.

On top of his desk was a picture of him and Pam at their graduation dance. *Lord, she was beautiful in that pink satin gown. Her hair curled just so. She didn't want me to run my fingers through it 'cause I'd mess it up. And that miserable tux was too warm.*

So much had happened since then, and he longed to be that carefree youth who was so sure of himself. *I guess, after several years of being told what to do, I'll have to do that on my own now.* His eyelids slid closed, and his last thoughts were dreams.

****

Pam sat on the steps to the porch with their dog, Rinny, his head on her lap. Running her hand over the soft muzzle, she heard her mother. "Pam, was that Hank who brought you home? Where's Tom?"

"He had too much to drink." Rinny raised his head, and she scratched behind his ears. "Mom, I wonder about Tom. I think he still loves me, but he snapped at me tonight. And I never knew him to drink hard liquor, but he asked for a whiskey straight up, after having both champagne and beer."

"Honey, I think being in combat changes men. Your father was different when he came back from the Great War, in 1918. He was not the boy who went off to fight in the glorious battle."

"What happened?"

She sighed and sat beside Pam. "We lived in Wisconsin then. Like you, I had known your father most of my life. He was high-spirited and fancy-free when he was a boy. When he came home after the war was over, he was serious and quiet. There were his nightmares of trench warfare that used to wake me after we were married—and still do, occasionally." She paused. "One thing didn't change. He still loved me. I got used to the new man. You'll learn to love the new Tom, but there will be challenges, too."

"I hope I can handle the problems."

Her mother smiled. "Just stand firmly by him and love him. That's all he needs right now."

They stood and turned toward the door. As they reached it, Rinny made a low growl in his throat, and his hackles rose as he faced the driveway.

Pam pursed her lips. "What's wrong, boy?"

Rinny gave a small woof, sniffed the air, and

then trotted to the hedges to check around before he came back to the porch.

Her mother shrugged. "It must have been an animal."

Looking out into the night, Pam wasn't so sure.

Chapter 17

"Dad?" Tom put his hand on his father's shoulder in the projection booth. When his dad looked up, Tom continued, "I'm sorry for what I said last night. It felt good to pity myself."

Hesitating a moment as Jenny walked through the lobby, Dad gave a quick nod. "Accepted. You know, Jenny's the one who really came out of this the worst." He swallowed a couple of times, tears in his eyes. "I don't know what I'd do if I lost your mother. And I came very close, when those gangsters tried to kill her."

Tom pursed his lips as he thought about Pam. "At least we're still here and breathing. She's so brave to go on."

Heading back into the restaurant, Tom thought about things. Pam had arrived a few minutes before and was cleaning off the bar. When their eyes met, she looked down. *Dear God, how much of an ass was I last night?* Sliding behind the bar, he put his arms around her and that ever-present tingle when he was around her coursed in his insides. She didn't stiffen, so he must still be in her good graces.

Snuggling into his embrace, she ventured, "You seem in good spirits this afternoon."

His breath stirred her hair as he spoke in her ear. "I'm sorry about yesterday. I guess going back to being a civilian isn't as easy as I thought."

Pushing back, she gazed at him. "I'm here if you need me. I know you've been through a lot and it still bothers you that you can't dance the way you used to. I shouldn't have danced with Hank and left you sitting there."

Tom shook his head. "That's not important. I have to get used to it. Lord knows, many men were hurt far worse." He looked around. "Can you get away for a while?"

Pam hesitated. "I guess. As long as I can be here in about an hour."

Tom called into the kitchen. "Jenny, Pam and I need to talk. Can you spare her?"

Coming into the restaurant, Jenny waved. "As long as she's back in time to set up the liquor."

"I'll help her."

Something strongly resembling her old impish smile crossed her face. "How can I say no?"

Tom clamped onto Pam's arm. "Good. Come on!" Leading her to the stairs that went to the second floor over the theater, he asked, "Ever been all the way up?"

Pam's puzzlement was evident. "No. Why?"

"It's private. No one comes up unless something's wrong with the electric sign."

At the top, Pam gazed around in wonder. There was a line of doors down the hall and a set of stairs at the other end. "I thought this was a storage area up here. What are all these rooms?"

"When my family first came to Juneau, my parents lived in the apartment next to the office and all the others working on the theater lived up here. The last door on the right is a bathroom with a tub." He opened the door to a corner room. "This was my Aunt Muriel's room when Jenny was a baby."

Pam exclaimed over the cheery room with the two big windows and, from one of them, a view of the harbor. An old-fashioned washstand and bureau of dark wood stood on one side of the room, a bed with a large sheet over it was on the other, and another sheet covered the piece of furniture gracing the front window. Pulling the sheet off the seat of an old wicker loveseat, Tom bowed with a flourish. "Have a seat, m'lady."

It squeaked as they sat, and it smelled dusty from years of disuse. Tom put his arm around her shoulder. "When should we set the date?"

"You're invited to our house for dinner this Sunday, along with your parents, and we'll plan it out. Where do you want to live?"

"I brought you up here for a reason. We could live up here until we find a place of our own."

Pam silently looked around. "It feels romantic to live above a theater. And this is such a pretty room. I think I could stand it for a while. Did you ask your family if it was all right?"

Tom laughed. "They suggested it. We can plan a house when we're ready." Catching a whiff of her perfume, desire grabbed him in its wake. Nuzzling her neck, he worked his way up behind her ear. A murmured sound of arousal escaped her lips, then she gently pushed him away.

With a hand on his chest, she said, "I think we should wait until after the wedding, now."

The frustrated male part of his psyche protested. "You didn't seem to mind the other times."

"I wasn't going to see you for awhile, then, and I knew you needed it. Think of it as a promise of a lifetime in a week or two."

He shifted, causing the wicker to comment. "I'll have to deal with an unrequited painful experience, but if it's your wish, I'll go along with it." A reluctant tone accented the statement, and he couldn't believe how much he wanted to whine.

Pam inspected the furniture in the room while Tom collected himself. When she pulled the sheet off the bed, her only comment was, "The things in here will have to be cleaned, but I think this will work well."

Tom headed to the door. "Come on, I'll help you

set up the bar."

As they went down the stairs, they heard shouts coming from the office area. "What the hell—?" Tom exclaimed as they raced toward the office door. It burst open just as they reached it, and they could see Tom's dad and Uncle Josh slapping each other on the back and "hoo-hawing," while his mother and Aunt Muriel hugged each other. Tom watched them, amazed. "What's all the hubbub?"

The rest of the family, brought by all the noise, piled up behind Tom and Pam, waiting for an answer while Dad wiped his eyes. "We got a long distance call from Dan Hanson. The producers of the musical got in touch with him. They want him to direct a movie version of *Gold Rush* and wanted him to call us for our permission!"

The collective group howled in unison, and Jenny hugged her father. "That's wonderful news! What else did he say?"

Uncle Josh took up the story. "They want Em and Dave to play the leads, and Zeke and me to go to the studio as consultants and musical directors."

His mother and Aunt Muriel took Tom and Hank aside with Mom putting her arm around Tom. "Since you and Hank are back, do you think you could run the theater if Muriel and I go to Hollywood with them?"

Muriel added, "Jen is already running the restaurant and bar. You'll have Ivan to help you, and Scott and Don haven't got new jobs yet." She looked at them both, her eyes hopeful.

Hank grinned at Tom. "Do you hear a 'puh-leeze' coming on?"

Tom shook his head. "I suppose we can forego our future and let you go make a movie." He turned to his mother. "And I'll bet you land a role in it, if I know you."

Smacking him on the chest, she retorted, "You

sound like your father."

"By the way, Mom, Pam liked the idea of fixing up the corner room upstairs and living there until we can afford a house."

Muriel nodded. "That's the best room up there. Use as many rooms as you want. And you and Pam will be right here, anyway."

Mom smiled. "No one has lived here since we all moved out, over twenty years ago. Watch out for the ghosts."

"Ghosts?" Pam exclaimed as she walked up from behind.

Putting his arms around her, Tom said, "Don't you know, all old theaters have ghosts? Worry not—I have my sword of truth and shield of righteousness."

Hank folded his arms. "I thought that only worked in Bugs Bunny cartoons."

Enjoying a good laugh, they took off to their respective jobs to make their plans. Tom helped Pam restock the bar, all the while trying to make her sorry she'd rebuffed him.

****

Pam helped her mother set the table while they waited for Tom and his parents to join them. Ted had decided his girlfriend was better company than the rest of the family planning for a wedding, so he was out for the evening. The plates in Pam's hand shook as the realization hit her that her dream of being Mrs. Tom Shafer would soon be here.

She finished setting the table and headed for the front door. "I'm going to wait on the porch."

Fall's scent was in the air. Leaves were turning glorious colors against the dark green of the hemlocks on the mountainside, and fall flowers added a glowing splash. Pam moved out onto the porch, and the crisp wind caressed her. What a beautiful time to be married. Sitting on the porch railing, she rested her back against the corner post.

Rinny sat next to her and nudged her leg with his nose, and she scratched his ears. "I'm going to miss you, boy. I can't take you to the theater. Maybe someday, when we get a house..."

Hearing a car pull up in the driveway, Pam slid down from the railing and stood at the top of the steps with Rinny beside her. As he observed the people getting out of the car, his tail started moving slowly. Hurrying up first, Tom stroked the dog's head, which sent Rinny into a doggie smile. "Yeah, you know me, don't you, boy?" Straightening, he took Pam into his arms. "No bite here, either?"

She gave him a sideways grin. "Perhaps." Then she was lost in a kiss that made her toes tingle. When she was able to take a breath, Zeke and Addy were on their way up the steps, and Rinny gave them each an identifying sniff before he sat by Pam, looking at her expectantly. The hostess in her led them to the door after she greeted them.

Her father, Zeke, and Tom settled into the living room while Pam and Addy headed to the kitchen. Pam's mother finished putting the mashed potatoes into the china serving bowl as Addy said, "Can I help you with anything?"

"I just need to get everything to the table."

The three women picked up dishes heaped with food and took them into the dining room, and in no time the table was loaded with the feast, while the men followed their noses. Tom held a chair for Pam, then sat next to her as her mother made an entrance carrying the crown of pork roast with baked apples in the center, and the aroma made Pam's stomach growl. Setting it in the middle of the table, Mom smiled. "I'm glad there's no more rationing."

After grace and the passing of dishes, Pam's father looked at her. "Pam, did you speak to the pastor about the church?"

She sighed. "Yes. It seems so many couples are

planning to get married this month that we can't have the church."

Addy took up the subject. "I asked, and he *could* come over to the restaurant for a few hours. We can have the wedding and reception there."

Putting his fork down, Pam's dad emphasized, "Of course, we'll pay for the food and your time."

Addy and Zeke glanced at each other, and then Zeke spoke up. "I know it's traditional for the bride's family to pay, but I think we should halve it."

The negotiations went on until the last bit of ice cream dessert was consumed. The date was set for the next Saturday, because Pam wanted time for Kata to finish the wedding gown, and then decorations, scheduling, and the multitude of other necessary details were decided.

The last light of day made giant shadows along the grass of the backyard, and the crisp fall breeze played around Pam and Tom as they escaped the house. Their parents started a game of bridge around the card table in the living room while listening to Jack Benny on the radio. Pam sat on the plank bench in the rose garden, and Tom settled with her, his arm around her shoulders.

He gazed at her in such a way it made her heart flutter. "I want to talk to you about our future. I've decided what I want to do, and of course you need to know. After Hank and I run Golden North for the folks when they go to Hollywood, I'd like to look for work as an airline pilot. I'll keep in practice by working for your father, running the mail again. One thing I must tell you is that a job like that could take us away from here. Are you willing to move, to go where the jobs are?"

Pam hesitated, then sighed. "I hate the thought of leaving the only home I've ever known, but if that's what we have to do, I'll go with you. You and any children we have are my family now."

"I have money saved up from my pay in the army. We could probably get a nice house wherever we go."

Pam nodded. "I haven't spent much from the money I've made, either. I'm sure we have enough to start out. Did your parents say how long they think the movie will take?"

"They estimated about a year. Living at the theater, we'll be saved the expense of a place to live. Dad and Uncle Josh said Hank and I can split the take between us while they're gone. I'm sure the movie company will pay well. And, hopefully, they won't run into the Giovannis there."

She straightened and looked him in the eyes. "I hope they'll be all right when they go to Hollywood for the movie."

He shook his head. "That was over long ago. They'll be fine." Drawing her back to him, he told her, "This is what I dreamed of during all those years of war. Now I have you in my arms forever. I even named my airplane 'Alaskan Angel.' I knew you'd watch over me."

Raw emotion surged through her. To be so loved! How had she ever doubted him? "I feel so safe and secure with you." Her head was on his chest, the breeze lightly teasing her hair, and he put both arms around her while they stayed and watched the stars pop out of the twilight. A few minutes later, they strolled arm in arm toward the house.

The following Thursday, Pam went earlier than usual to the restaurant. As they finished setting up, she told Jenny, "I'm walking again to the Nikolaevichs' for Kata to finish the alterations on my wedding dress."

"The fog's pretty thick today. I could ask someone to drive you over."

"No, everyone's busy right now. Anyway, I've been walking over there for three days in a row, and they only live four blocks away. I should be back in an hour." With that, Pam was out the lobby doors.

The gray harbor fog floated around in great puffs, leaving drops of moisture on her face. She didn't mind it much. It made her think of the mysteries she'd read that were set in London, and she almost expected to meet up with Holmes or Watson strolling along the street. The alleys between buildings looked shadowy and eerie, and she hummed to herself nervously as she crossed one of the drives that headed into the back of the buildings.

Suddenly, Pam felt a grab to her shoulder, but before she could react, a strong hand clamped a foul-smelling cloth to her face. Feebly trying to struggle, she felt her thumb break the chain on her locket, but before she could claw at that hand, darkness descended over her.

Chapter 18

Struggling down the stairs with the empty paint cans, Tom took them through the lobby and into the restaurant. He had on his old overalls and a tattered flannel shirt with the sleeves rolled up.

Jenny attacked him. "Don't bring those messy things in here! Why didn't you take them down the back stairs?"

"Didn't think of it. I'll take them out back to the trash." He hauled them to the garbage area and returned to the restaurant, where Jenny was finishing up the table settings. "Hank and I left the windows open a little in that room. It might not help dry the paint much, with this fog, but at least it will let some of the smell out. Remind me to close it up before we go home." He looked around. "Where's Pam?"

"She left to go to the Nikolaevichs' about—"—She glanced at her watch—"—a half-hour ago. I think this was the last of her alterations." Heading for the kitchen, she turned. "That reminds me. I need to check on the supplies for Saturday."

Tom went to the bar and tapped some of the ice water into a glass, then sat at one of the tables and put his feet up on the seat of the chair beside him.

When his mother came in from the office, her comment was immediate.

"I hope you cleaned up first."

"All the paint is on the front. Don't worry."

Giving him the evil eye, she pointed. "Did you bring a change of clothes?"

He sighed. "I'll go change after I drink the

water. Hank's cleaning the brushes, out in back."

Mom went on to the lobby, and then Tom heard the door swing open with a murmur of voices as she returned with Kata Nikolaevich. "Tom, did Pam leave to go for her alterations?"

"I was upstairs when she left." He called toward the kitchen. "Jenny?"

Jenny came in with a pad of paper in her hand. "What is it?"

"You said Pam left here about a half-hour ago?"

"Yes, to go for the alterations." She stopped when she saw Kata. "What—?"

Feeling the hair prickle on the back of his neck, Tom exclaimed, "She should have been there by now."

Kata looked thoughtful. "Maybe she stopped in a store on the way over."

Jenny shook her head. "That doesn't sound like Pam. She's usually prompt for any appointment."

Mounting concern pounded in his chest and ears. "She wouldn't have become disoriented in the fog. She knows her way around." Thinking for a moment, he said, "Jenny, are you free for a while?"

She nodded. "Why?"

"I want to trace her route. Let's see if we can find her. She might have fallen." He was grasping at anything to explain this.

Jenny retrieved their jackets, and they set out. "Pam usually heads that way."

Pointing to the ground, he started scanning. "Keep an eye out for anything."

The fog closed around them like a blanket, and shadows of things seemed to move by the buildings. They crossed the first street without seeing a soul, and then a car crept by, its headlights reflecting off the wall of gray mist. Jenny stayed along the sides of the buildings and Tom searched the street edge.

Coming to the drive into the alley in the second

block, Jenny gasped. "Tom, look at this." She was pointing to something shiny next to one of the garbage cans.

He went to inspect it. "It looks like someone lost a locket."

Jenny hugged herself. "It's Pam's. I'm sure of it."

Opening the small heart, the necklace shook in his hand. "That's my picture in there." He leaned against the sturdy bricks. "What the hell?"

Traversing the alley until they were mid-block, Jenny shook her head. "What could have happened to her?"

"I wonder if someone hit her with a car and took her to the hospital?" He sprinted out of the alley with Jenny right behind him. They made it back to the theater in seconds, and Tom raced to the office. His Uncle Josh was behind the desk going over promotional material. "Uncle Josh, may I use the phone to call the hospital?"

Josh sucked in a breath. "What happened?"

Tom had the phone book out and was thumbing down the pages as Jenny told what they'd found.

Josh moved out of his chair. "Help yourself."

Tom underlined the number and dialed the phone quickly. When the nurse at the hospital answered, he said, "Hello? This is Tom Shafer. I want to know if you've had anyone come in to emergency in the last hour."

"Just a moment, I'll check."

"Thank you." Putting his hand over the receiver. "They're checking," he said to the group assembled.

After a few minutes, the nurse came back. "Mr. Shafer?"

"Yes?"

"I'm sorry, no one has been admitted to the hospital since last night."

"No one? You're sure?"

"I double-checked."

"Okay, thanks." Returning the receiver to the cradle, he stared at his family, speechless.

Jenny took a breath. "Well, she couldn't have fallen off the face of the earth. Do you think it's possible she felt sick and walked home?"

Tom's mother shook her head. "If that were the case, I'm sure she would have returned here for someone to take her home."

Sitting back in the chair, Tom said, "I thought of calling her mother, but I don't want to worry her."

Josh sat on the edge of the desk. "I wonder if we should call the sheriff?"

Silence descended over the group. Jenny spoke up. "Dad, do you think it's a matter for the law?"

"I don't know who else to turn to. I don't know if we can call it a missing person case, but it seems to me the sooner we start looking, the better."

Opening the phone book again, Tom called the sheriff's office. As he replaced the receiver, he said, "Sheriff Lindsey will be over in a few minutes."

The somber group filed into the restaurant, where Tom sat at one of the tables and Jenny put her arms around him. "I know you're thinking the worst, but I'm sure we'll find her."

He patted her hand. "Thank you, cuz."

When the sheriff arrived, everyone gave an account of the events of the last hour, and then he flipped the notepad closed. "No one has informed the Wrights yet?" At the negative replies, he continued, "Tom, show me the place where you found the locket. Then I'll take you to the Wrights' house, if you want to be the one to tell them."

Tom looked questioningly at the others. "Mr. Wright won't be home."

Tom's dad came forward. "I'll call him at the airfield."

Lindsey tapped his notebook on his chin. "I can run to the airfield after I drop Tom off."

Putting his hand on the sheriff's shoulder, Tom said, "Tell him not to call home until I can tell Mrs. Wright myself. I'll stay with her until Mr. Wright gets home. Let me change clothes before I go. I don't want to tell Mrs. Wright with me looking like a street urchin." Turning to Hank. "Could you take care of the upstairs room for me?"

Hank clapped him on the shoulder. "Sure will."

After a quick clean-up and change, Tom went out the lobby doors with the sheriff and hopped into the patrol car's passenger side. "I haven't been in here since—" He suddenly went cold.

Lindsey glanced over and picked up his thought. "Since you were attacked by Vic Houston? Tom, do you think Vic has something to do with this?"

Tom stared ahead. "I don't even know if Vic ever made it back to Juneau from the war."

Lindsey pursed his lips. "I could find out. He did seem to have a fixation on Miss Wright. Now, was this the alley you found the locket in?"

Getting out of the car with the sheriff behind him, he pointed to the spot by the wall of the building. "We found it right there."

Lindsey pulled out his flashlight and inspected the area. "Did you or Mrs. Marshall walk along here?"

"No. We stayed to the middle after we retrieved the locket."

He indicated with the flashlight. "There seems to have been a scuffle here by the wall. You didn't see anything down the alley?" Tom shook his head. "He must have had a car with him."

Tom's brain raged. *My God, did Vic have something to do with this? And after I saved his miserable ass.* He jumped when Lindsey put his hand on his shoulder.

"Boy, we can't think the worst right now. That's what Sheriff Amos used to say. I promise you, I'll do everything in my power to get Pam back to you."

As he gave Tom a lift to the Wrights' house, Lindsey said, "I'll tell Bill you're going to stay here. And don't worry, Tom, I'm going to get right on this case."

Taking a deep breath, Tom wished he didn't have to tell Mrs. Wright this news. He pushed the doorbell and hoped the ground would swallow him up. She came to the door wiping her hands on an apron. "Why, Tom, what are you doing here?"

Tom clasped her hands. "Come with me to the living room. You'd better sit down."

Concern filled her blue eyes. "What's wrong?"

He sighed. "Pam set out today to the Nikolaevichs' and never got there. She's missing. Jenny and I found her locket by a building in an alley, and the sheriff said there were signs of a scuffle."

"But who would—?" Suddenly, her eyes grew round. "Oh, no! You don't think it was Vic?"

Tom pursed his lips. "We think it might be."

"Oh, my. What would he do to her?" She dissolved into tears, and Tom put his arms around her.

"Pam is very smart. I'm sure she will be all right." Tom silently prayed this to be true while he fixed Mrs. Wright some coffee and they waited for Mr. Wright.

****

Pam had no idea where she was. Even before she opened her eyes she heard the song of wind through pines and smelled both the salt breeze and the hemlock trees. Her head felt two sizes too big, and she was nauseous. *That smell. Now, I know what it is. Ether. I remember the smell from when I had my tonsils out when I was seven.* She took several deep breaths and opened her eyes, clearing her mind.

Gazing carefully around, she could see she was on a bed in a small, pine-walled room, with a window up behind her. Nothing else was there except a plain wooden dining armchair, and as her senses came to her, Pam's stomach began to tense with fear spreading out through her system. *Where am I? And how on earth did I get here?* She moved to sit up, but the effects of the ether hit her and her head spun. Closing her eyes again, she put her hand over her face, gaining equilibrium. After several more deep breaths, she tried again and managed to swing her right leg over the side of the bed. Her ankle felt strangely heavy, and she glanced down, only to suck in a terrified whimper. There was a hinged iron ring padlocked together, with a long length of chain attached to it. She was shackled to the wall.

A large form filled the door frame, and she swallowed a frightened scream, trying to calm herself. As the man stepped closer she recognized his features: it was Vic Houston. In a voice that sounded like a croak, she asked, "Why did you do this? Where am I?"

He smirked. "Just rescuing you from yerself, darlin'. I saw the announcement in the paper." He leaned over her and said in her face, "You don't know what yer doin'."

I've got to stay calm until Tom can find me. She crammed resolve into her brain. "I'm very aware what I'm doing. You, on the other hand, don't seem to realize that this is a serious crime of abduction."

"I'm like the cavalry saving the gal from the—wild injins." He chortled at his own joke.

"If you're saving me, why am I shackled to the wall?"

"'Cause you don't believe I'm the best thing for you that ever came down the pike." He took her hand, and she tried desperately not to flinch. "I gave

198

you enough chain to reach the bathroom, and the kitchen when I'm at work." He hauled her up. "I'll show you around."

The leg ring rubbed painfully on her ankle as Pam followed him out of the room. From the dark hallway, Vic opened a door at the end to a rustic bath with half-century-old fixtures. The smell of mold was strong. The little window, painted shut long before, showed nothing but woods beyond.

Going down the hall in the other direction, they turned to the right, into a tiled kitchen. It wasn't very modern, either. An old gas range and refrigerator were on one side, and a freestanding sink next to a dropleaf table with two wooden chairs, mates to the one in the bedroom, were on the other. Pam edged toward the door at the end of the room, but the chain drew her up short.

Vic chuckled. "Ya see, I measured it very carefully. You can't make it out any of the doors."

Pam's fear was replaced by anger. "How long do you plan to keep me like this?"

Walking slowly toward her, he hissed, "Until you come to your senses." His hand moved as if to touch her. "You're mine now."

Slapping his hand away, she retorted, "Don't you dare touch me, or I'll fight tooth and nail. You'll be so sorry..."

He put both his arms up in surrender. "I can wait. You'll have enough time to think. Hours and hours." Grabbing his jacket, he went out the door. Pam heard an engine fire and go away.

She went into the bath and used the facilities, and then she took stock of her situation. Passing the kitchen, she found the chain wasn't long enough to reach to the living area, and she saw why. There was an old phone on a desk there.

Now she had a goal.

Heading back to the bedroom, she studied how

the chain was attached. It was bolted onto the wooden wall, and if she could find something to pry with, maybe she could pull it out.

She set out to explore the cabin areas she could reach.

Chapter 19

When Pam's father arrived home, Tom met him at the door. The sheriff had brought Mr. Wright up to date on what he was going to do to find Pam, and Tom's mind whirled with what Pam would be going through. *Sweetheart, stay brave. I'll be coming for you as soon as I can.*

His Aunt Muriel answered the phone when Tom called the theater. He let her know Mr. Wright had gotten home and then asked, "What's going on over there?"

"The sheriff just got back from talking to Vic. He'll wait until you get here to tell us what he found." Just then Pam's brother Ted came in and gave Tom a wave.

"I'll ask Mr. Wright if he can give me a lift." Tom said. "Ted just came in the door. He can probably stay with his mother." Tom hung up and turned to Mr. Wright with the latest information.

"Sure, I'll give you a lift to the theater."

They quickly filled Ted in about what had happened to Pam, and he agreed to stay with his mother, waiting for further news.

In a couple of minutes Tom was sliding into the passenger seat of the Buick and they were off to the theater. Hurrying through the lobby doors, they ran into Ivan, who sent them to the restaurant.

For the few hours before opening, they'd arranged some chairs together, and Tom at first sat with Mr. Wright in the remaining unoccupied ones. His parents, aunt and uncle, Jenny, Hank, and Kata were there, and next to Kata was her cousin, Sarah

Darcy.

Popping back onto his feet, Tom held out a hand to Sarah. "Mrs. Darcy, it's wonderful to see you again. Are you here to help us?"

Sarah smiled. "I'll see what I can do."

Clearing his throat, Sam said, "I, too, am glad to see you, again," but his tone was one of reluctance.

Sarah glanced at him. "I promise I won't get in your way, Sam. Kata wanted me to help on this side of the fence."

"Where's Amos?"

"He's working on a case for one of our clients in Skagway. Got to keep our detective agency going." She chuckled.

When Tom sat again, Sam started his report. "I found Vic got his job back at the service station after his military service, so I questioned him there. He said he gave up on trying to win over Miss Wright and he hadn't seen her since he got back from fighting in Europe."

Tom shook his head. "Sheriff, he was fighting here in the Pacific. I know, because I saw him at Fort Myers myself."

"He said he was transferred to France after the battle on Kiska."

Tom's mother looked thoughtful and suddenly repeated, "Europe, Europe..." Then she grabbed Aunt Muriel by the arm and pulled her toward the office, saying, "We have to look for that envelope!"

"What envelope?" Muriel managed to say before the door slammed behind them.

Sarah spoke up. "Does he still live at home?"

"No. He has an apartment over the grocery store. And, before you ask, I'm getting a search warrant for it tomorrow. The judge is out of town, so we have to wait. I plan to talk to Vic's parents tomorrow, as well."

Tom jumped up. "Can't you do that now? There's

no telling what Vic will do to her."

Coming over to Tom, Sam patted him on the back. "Son, the legal investigation takes time. To do it right, we have to do it within the law."

Mr. Wright nodded. "We have to put Pam's well-being in God's hands." He glanced at Tom. "I don't like her being abducted any more than you do, but I want her returned safe, and I want any charges brought against her abductor to stick."

There was a shout of triumph from the office, followed by Aunt Muriel and Mom dashing out, Mom waving an envelope in her hand, to approach the sheriff. Mom handed the envelope to him. "I almost forgot about this. It came to Pam right after the German surrender a few months ago."

Pulling the slip of paper out of the envelope, Sam gave it a glance and then handed it to Sarah. "Soon?"

Mom nodded. "You can see it isn't signed, and there's no indication on the envelope where it's from, except for 'APO Europe.'"

Sam shoved it into his pocket. "I'll see if this is his writing. If it is, we may have some important evidence."

Tapping her foot, Sarah directed her gaze at the sheriff. "Sam, I was thinking, one of us should check with Vic's parents at the same time the other searches his apartment. If he has two places to hide Pam, he might just transport her from one to the other while we investigate."

Sam looked thoughtful. "What about the service station?"

Sarah shook her head. "It's too open, and people come and go all the time."

"Good idea." He turned to the others. "We'll tell you tomorrow what we've found."

Tom spoke up. "If there's anything I can do, let me know."

The sheriff gripped Tom's shoulder. "Don't worry. We'll find out what's happened to her."

Tom's stomach was in several knots as he sent up a prayer for her safety. *Lord, let us find her before Vic does anything to harm her, because if he does, I'll kill him, sure as I'm standing here.* The soldier in him had taken over.

****

Pam pounded another nail between the double bracket and the wall that held her shackle chain, and there was a satisfying crack. She counted only four more long nails in the old box she'd found in the kitchen. Her mallet was fashioned out of a wooden kitchen spoon and a large metal nut found in the bathroom. Pam had worked the loose nut off the base of the toilet and then jammed the nut onto the end of the spoon, and it made a serviceable hammer.

She looked around for something she could use as a pry bar. Suddenly, she heard a vehicle drive up, and she hurriedly stashed her tools between the mattress and box springs, dragging the chair over in front of the bracket.

Pouring herself some coffee in the kitchen, she didn't look up when Vic came in the door, greeting her with, "Hello, darlin'. I brought you some groceries. You're gonna be here a while."

She turned a cold eye on him. "What do you mean by that?"

He gave her an oily smile. "As soon as you agree to marry me, you're free."

"I'm already engaged to someone else, and the wedding is set."

Coming nose to nose with her, he growled, "There ain't gonna be a wedding without a bride. I aim to keep you here until you change your mind."

She pushed him away. "I'm not going to."

"Don't worry, I'm not gonna take you here. Things will be good and proper. You stay here by yourself until you agree. Probably won't be long."

"Why?"

"This cabin is far into the woods. No one knows where you are. I'll check on you every morning and every afternoon." He laughed. "Until you become *my* wife."

A chill went up her spine. There was no telling what would happen to her at night—if someone broke in, or if there was a fire—

He took a step toward her. "Now give me a kiss and I'll be on my way."

"Don't you dare touch me." She waved the hot coffeepot at him.

Vic backed to the kitchen door. "I'll give it time, darlin'. In a few days you'll be begging to marry me, just to get out of here." The door slammed, and then she heard him drive away.

Pam stood drawing deep breaths to quell the panic that was threatening to overwhelm her. *Have to think clearly. Where am I? Can Tom or the law be able to find me? I must not be too far from town, but where? If I got away, would I get lost?* As calmly as she could, she started searching for something to pry that damned chain out of the wall.

Chapter 20

Tom picked up Mrs. Wright the next morning to be at the restaurant when the sheriff and Sarah came to report their findings. As she settled into the passenger seat, Mrs. Wright handed Tom an envelope. "I found this in Pam's desk, where she has all the letters you sent during the war. I have no idea why she saved it, but it may be an important clue."

He looked at the address. "This seems to be the same handwriting that was on the other envelope, the one my mother had. I remember this. Pam showed it to me and asked me about what it said. How could I forget? I was so ashamed of myself."

Hesitating, she said, "That was a couple of years ago."

Tom flushed. "Vic must have sent this one, as well."

Mrs. Wright patted his arm. "I know that was settled long ago. I don't hold one indiscretion against you. I do believe you love Pam and wouldn't hurt her."

With a determined set to his jaw, Tom drove off toward the theater. "I couldn't live without her now. We have to find her and bring her home." His fist hit the steering wheel for emphasis.

His family, Kata, Sarah, and Sheriff Sam were waiting at the restaurant when Tom and Mrs. Wright arrived. Tom slid into the seat next to his mother, and Mrs. Wright gave the sheriff the envelope, telling him about it before she sat beside Tom.

Checking the new envelope with the other, Sam glanced up. "Mrs. Wright, it seems to be a match. This will prove that Vic has been after her for some time."

Tom spoke up. "Millie can verify that Vic was harassing Pam when she was a waitress there."

Sarah nodded. "We've already talked to her."

The sheriff waved his hand. "Sarah went to see Vic's parents this morning, while I went through his apartment. We didn't find Miss Wright, but I learned something from his landlady, who has an apartment on the ground floor. It seems Mr. Houston got back from work forty-five minutes after he usually does, having left work at the usual time. And, he left to go to work an hour earlier this morning."

Sarah took it up. "His parents told me he had borrowed some of their old furniture and supplies in the past two weeks. He said it was for his apartment."

The sheriff moved to Tom. "We thought we would tail him after work, to see where he goes, but Sarah had an idea. If we follow him in a car and he sees us, he might get suspicious, so if we can give you a signal, maybe you and Sarah could tail him in a plane."

Sarah put her hand on Tom's shoulder. "We could stay far enough up that Vic wouldn't notice us."

Tom pursed his lips. "How would we know that we were following the right car?"

Sarah grinned. "I'll put a white paint streak on the top. He shouldn't notice it, when he gets in the car."

"How do we know when he's on the move?"

Sam gazed thoughtfully at Tom. "Do you think you could tune into the police frequency on the airplane's radio?"

"If you give me the number, I could."

"Good. I'll stake out the service station and signal you when he leaves work. Then you can tell me where he's going." Turning to them all, Sam said, "I believe he gets off work around five, so we have a few hours to set up. Tom, do you think there will be any problem borrowing a mail plane?"

"With Mr. Wright in charge? No."

"Okay, you and Sarah be at the airfield by four-thirty."

Tom's built-in response to taking orders kicked in. He was sure this was going to work, and, by God, he'd see that it did—Pam's life depended on it, and she needed him to think clearly.

As Tom had thought, there was no problem taking the extra mail plane. Sarah gave him the frequency of the police band, and they were soon talking to the sheriff. Sarah had gone to the service station earlier with a small can of paint and, unnoticed, had put a visible white stripe in the middle of the black car's roof.

At a quarter to five, the sheriff's voice crackled through the radio. "Mr. Houston just got into his car. He didn't seem to notice the paint on the roof. He's in too much of a hurry. Get the plane up."

Tom and Sarah had been seated in the plane for ten minutes, and now Tom switched on the engine and got a hand signal from Mr. Wright that it was safe to take off. They taxied onto the runway and soon the small plane was airborne.

Sarah handled the radio. "Did you see which way he went?"

"He turned down Front Street, then headed north."

Turning the small plane toward town, Tom spotted the black car with the white stripe pulling into a parking lot on Gold, and Sarah thumbed the mike. "Sam, he pulled into the grocery store on Gold.

We won't be able to hover. Could you put a stake on the grocery store and tell us when he's on the move again?"

"Ten-four, Sarah. Heading over there now. Will let you two know."

Tom turned the small plane off over the channel, where the water glistened in the evening sun. The days were getting shorter; soon it would be dark at this hour.

Sarah glanced at Tom. "I heard your folks are going back to Hollywood for a while."

He nodded. "Dad and Uncle Josh are going to be the musical directors on the film of their play. I think my mom and my aunt are going back for old times' sake."

"Are they worried at all about the Giovannis?"

"That was long ago. I don't think they'll have to hide out."

Suddenly, the radio came to life. "Tom, Sarah, Vic's on the move again."

Sarah came back. "We're on our way."

Quickly spotting the car, Tom kept well back so as not to be detected. "He's turned onto Basin Road, headed toward the dead end."

Sarah checked out the window. "He's turning in on a dirt drive, north about a half-mile from the end of the road. There's a broken wagon wheel to the west of it." Letting go of the mike, she took out a pair of binoculars and asked Tom, "Could you fly so I can see the lot number on the driveway?" After she jotted down the number, she thumbed the mike again and gave it to Sam.

"Got it, Sarah. I'll get a warrant and then meet you back at the theater as soon as possible."

"Ten-four, Sam."

Flying back to the airfield, Tom turned to Sarah. "Isn't the sheriff going to drive over there?"

Sarah put a hand on his shoulder. "Several of us

have to go together with the warrant. It will be safer for Pam."

A dark cloud of doubt hung over him as they landed. *How long is this going to take?* Once in his dad's car, he wasted no time getting Sarah back to the theater, where Sam was waiting for them, legal paper in hand.

The sheriff waved Sarah into the patrol car. "Come on, you can guide us. I want to stop at the office first to pick up weapons."

Standing by his dad as the patrol car turned the corner, Tom watched it go, then bolted toward the station wagon. "Dad, I'm going too."

In no time Dad had grabbed Tom's arm. "No, you're not. Let the law do its job."

"You told me Mom was almost killed by those gangsters. Did you stand by and wait, or did you go to her?"

Looking thunderstruck, Dad sighed. "Go, but be safe."

Grabbing his cane, Tom jumped into the car, started it, and dashed off, turning the corner on two wheels. *He'd better not have touched her, or I will kill him.*

****

Pam put all her weight on the iron frying pan, forcing the handle behind the brace for the chain while she held onto the chair for balance. It had been several hours' work, but now she heard a number of loud cracks, finally. Then, suddenly, the pan came away from the wall and with it the brace, still bolted to a broken chunk of wallboard. Her feet slipped off the pan and hit the floor awkwardly, but she managed to steady herself with the chair and stay upright. Picking up the brace, she laughed at her little victory.

She gathered up the long chain as best she could and hurried to the living room's telephone, a length of chain still trailing behind her. When she heard a car coming down the dirt drive, her urgency grew. She grabbed the receiver and pounded on the cradle buttons. Nothing. *Oh, no! The lines have been cut. Now what do I do?*

At the sounds of Vic coming into the kitchen, panic overtook her reason, and she burst out the front door. The shackle bounced painfully on her foot, but she ran as fast as she could. Past his car, she heard footsteps hurrying behind her, and then her foot was pulled out from under her. She fell face first into the wet pine needles.

Vic laughed. "Goin' somewhere, darlin'?" Glancing back, she saw him standing on the chain that had dragged behind her.

Frustrated tears blurred her eyes as she hit the wet ground with her fist. "You want me to stay and you treat me like this? I don't want to be anywhere near you!" she rasped.

He came and pulled her up while she fought him. Exhausted, she knew he was too strong for her to win, but she had to try. Jerking her arms behind her, he marched her back to the cabin and, after shoving her onto the bed, wrapped the chain several times around the bedpost. "I'll be back in a few seconds. I'll be between you and both doors, so there's no way out for you."

Pam started fighting with the chain, but Vic was back almost immediately with a coil of rope. Yanking her up, he sat her on the chair as she clawed at him and kicked with her unshackled foot. They struggled for a while, but Pam tired first, and Vic secured both her arms to the arms of the chair and, winding the rope down her legs, managed to tie her feet together. He put the chain back around the leg of the bed.

Panting for a few moments, he finally said, "Looks like I'm going to have to make you dinner, sweetheart. The rope and chain should hold you."

Hearing the muffled squeak of the kitchen door, Vic jumped up and reached into his pocket to pull out a switchblade. The sharp metal clicked out of its casing when he thumbed it as he crept carefully toward the bedroom door. Pam held her breath.

Vic was almost to the hall when Tom appeared in the doorway. Pam cried out in fear for him, warning him of the knife, and Tom raised his cane in defense as he charged into the room.

Vic backed up, staying between Tom and Pam but moving and taunting Tom, with his back to her. She could see he wasn't paying any attention to her. Scooting her hips as far as she could to the edge of the chair, she managed to raise her feet and, as Vic stepped back into her range, she heaved her feet forward as hard as she could, her soles landing with force on his backside.

Vic's arms flailed, and his knife flew against the wall and skittered toward Tom, who picked it up. Sprawled on the floor, Vic cursed, then lunged at Tom's legs, knocking him off balance and onto the floor. The knife flew into the hall as Tom twisted, kicking the side of Vic's head. While Tom scrambled up, Vic plunged a fist into Tom's gut, and then the two of them were rolling around the floor, trading blows.

Pam held her breath, praying Tom would get the upper hand. He was on his back with Vic holding him down when Tom kicked up and flipped Vic into the wall, stunning him. Grabbing his cane, Tom hit Vic a hard blow on the crown, and Vic slumped against the bed.

Tom had raised the cane to hit him again when Pam screamed, "Tom, no!" He looked at her with an expression she'd never seen before. His eyes glowed crazy with rage, and she was scared.

"He's the enemy. I have to kill him!" Tom rasped.

"No! You hit him just now, and that was self-defense. You hit him again, that's murder!"

Standing over his prey, cane ready to bash Vic's brains out, Tom froze.

Pam continued, "You kill him, and you'll be the one to go to prison! You'll ruin our life together! Tom, think!" With every ounce of her being she appealed to the Tom she loved and remembered.

Slowly Tom let the cane drop to the floor, and Pam closed her eyes in sheer relief. When she opened them again, Tom had retrieved the knife and was on his way to cut her loose when they heard the sound of another car pulling up quickly outside. Vic had begun to stir as the sheriff appeared in the bedroom doorway.

"Tom, what the hell? You could have been killed!" Lindsey pulled Vic around from where he lay and slapped handcuffs on him. "What on earth possessed you to do this?"

Tom wiped his bloody nose on his sleeve and finished cutting Pam's bonds. "I'm sorry, Sheriff, but I couldn't just sit around and do nothing, with Pam's life at stake."

"What's with you Shafers, anyway? Your uncle was shot twenty-some years ago doing crazy heroics, too."

Sam inspected the padlock on Pam's leg ring while Sarah and one of the other deputies took Vic, fighting and cursing, into the kitchen. Leaning around the bedroom door, Sam called out, "Sarah! Find a padlock key on Houston."

Moments later, Sarah was unlocking the shackle. "You're free, Miss Wright."

Pam didn't know whether she could rise from the chair, she was shaking so badly. When she tried, her legs wouldn't hold her, and the terror she'd endured the last thirty-six hours overwhelmed her. Tom, love replacing in his eyes the rage that was

213

there moments before, had gently taken her arm to lead her out, and now she clung to him. He held her tight, stroking her hair and soothing her, as she wailed out her misery to him. She didn't want his tender hugs to end, and for the first time in days she felt safe.

They heard Vic being taken out, still cursing and pleading to see Pam, and then Sarah was with them.

Putting her hand on Tom's shoulder, Sarah said gently, "You should take her to the hospital, so they can check her out. You need to be checked out, too." She gave Tom his cane. "We've got to lock this building up. It's a crime scene."

Pam felt stronger now. Tom helped her into the station wagon, and they watched the sheriff pull out of the drive with Vic banging on the window of the patrol car. She breathed a ragged sigh.

Sliding behind the wheel, Tom started the engine, and they traveled in silence for a few moments. Finally he turned and glanced at her. "I'm sorry I tried to kill Vic. I guess because of my army training I convinced myself he was the enemy and had to die. Thank you for stopping me."

Pam stroked his arm. "I've never seen that look in your eyes before, and it scared me. If you'd killed him, you could have gone to prison."

"I need you to stop me if I ever do that again."

Hesitating a minute, Pam felt a swell of fear. "I want you to think before you start drinking a lot, too. That scares me, as well. I know some of the men who came home from the war have became regular drunks. I don't want that for you."

Taking her hand, he gave it a kiss. "I promise to try. Just let me know when I slip up."

She caressed his cheek. "Your eye is swelling some."

He laughed. "I've had worse."

Arriving at the hospital, Pam had some bruises to be taken care of, especially around her ankle. Tom's injuries were attended to, also, and then he dropped her off at her house to clean up and change while he did the same at his. When he picked her up a half-hour later, they arrived back at the theater to a hero's welcome.

The Shafers and the Wrights were all there and, shortly, Sheriff Sam and Sarah showed up.

Seeing them all assembled in the restaurant, Sam spoke to the interested crowd. "I gave all the information and evidence to the D.A. and he said we have an excellent chance to put away Mr. Houston for a long time." Pam squeezed Tom's hand.

Sarah nodded. "I found out from the Houstons that the cabin by Gold Creek was the family's hunting cabin, but they hadn't used it in years. Vic must have fixed it up after he came home from Europe. He's been planning this abduction for a long time."

Pam spoke up. "Where did he get the ether? I thought only hospitals used it."

"Auto mechanics use it. They spray it in the engine to help start a car," Sam answered. "So he took a can of it."

Mr. Wright shook the sheriff's hand. "Thank you for getting my daughter back." He glanced at Sarah, including her. "Both of you."

Sam waved a hand at Tom. "Even though I should skin him alive, Tom was the one who found and subdued Vic before we got there."

Tom put his arm around Pam. "I'd fight the devil himself if I thought Pam was in danger."

She kissed him on the cheek. "I love you, you know."

Kata came over to them. "I have your dress here in the dressing room area, and we only have a couple of adjustments to do. Why don't we do that in the morning before the ceremony?"

Pam nodded. "We'll be right on schedule, won't we?" The shadow of her old smile appeared.

Giving Pam a squeeze, Tom kissed her on her forehead. "Thank God, we got you back. Come on, I'll take you home."

Weary but happy, Pam walked on air next to her hero, while the sheriff and Sarah departed and everyone else disbursed to their own jobs.

Chapter 21

On his wedding morning, Tom was a burst of energy, getting furniture over to the theater and making sure the rooms were set for them to move in. They had waved the usual hotel suite in favor of the beautiful view on the theater's second floor.

Laughing, Hank plunked down the last chair. "I never figured you for a nesting instinct."

Tom stretched out on the divan in the living room. "I've got to do something besides pace, and I've got four hours to go."

"Sorry you missed your bachelor party Joe and I organized for you last night. It was a great time."

"Uh-huh, I'll bet it was. I needed some rest, after throttling Vic. And I've promised Pam I'll watch my drinking and my temper from now on."

"We've come by it honestly, from the tales we've been told about Grandpa Shafer."

Suddenly, they heard a commotion downstairs, and they hurried to the lobby. The family was greeting a well-dressed couple, and when the woman turned toward Tom, he exclaimed, "Em! Why didn't you tell me you were coming?" He gave her a hug.

She returned a sisterly embrace. "I wanted to surprise you. Anyway, I couldn't miss your wedding." Em pulled back with an I've-got-a-secret smile and motioned to the man standing behind her. Tom recognized Dave Kendall, her co-star. "We have another surprise. Dave and I got married in New York."

Tom frowned. "With none of us there? I don't recall you even telling us."

"It happened before we came back. We were in love and destined for movie fame in Hollywood, so we decided to hitch up before that."

"What did Mom and Dad say?"

She shrugged. "They were shocked, but, as Dad said, I'm of age."

Dave stood back waiting, and Tom put out his hand. "Welcome to the family, brother."

Nodding, Dave shook Tom's hand. "Thank you. And congratulations on your marriage to Pam. We wanted to be here today."

His parents came to Tom's side, and his mother laughed. "I always knew your sister was headstrong and impulsive."

Cocking his head at her, Tom ventured, "It must run in the family."

His dad howled and Mom gave him the evil eye while she waved her hand. "I'll remind you of that when your wedding pictures come back showing you with a black eye."

Absentmindedly, Tom put his hand to his face. "It's not that bad."

Slapping him on the back, Hank grabbed Tom's arm. "Come on, bruiser, it's time to put on the monkey suit." He stopped to give Em a kiss on the cheek and shake Dave's hand. "Congratulations from me, as well."

Tom and Hank slipped upstairs, where they'd stashed the tuxedos. They took turns in the tub shower and then fought their way into the formal suits.

Hank fixed the bowtie on Tom's collar while Tom grumbled, "This is worse than my dress uniform. At least I could move, in that."

Shrugging on his jacket, Hank checked himself in the mirror. "Looks good. Maybe one day I'll get the girl."

Tom poked him. "Not Mr. Confirmed Bachelor!

You'll play the field and run if one jumps at you."

Hank wiggled his eyebrows. "Sampling can be fun." He looked at his watch. "Time to go to your life sentence."

"No one ever went more willingly."

This was only the second time that Golden North was closed on a Saturday; the first had been when Jenny married. Today she would serve as Matron of Honor while Grandma Muriel took care of two-year-old Chase, who was often all over the restaurant at once.

Tom and Hank entered the dining room. Along the walls were the tables, which would be moved over into the room after the ceremony. The chairs stood in rows like soldiers, with an aisle down the middle. Overhead, the light fixtures were strung with red roses tied on gold and red crepe paper streamers, echoing the fall colors, while the bandstand at the front of the room glowed with red roses and fall leaves in an arch.

Tom blew out a nervous breath as Hank preceded him to the front. His dad, who would be playing the piano for the ceremony, clapped Tom on the back. "You've chosen a fine woman to bring into the family. I'm proud of you, son." Tom detected mist in his dad's eyes.

Embracing his father, Tom said, "Thank you, Dad."

Sitting at the front, the cousins conversed until people started settling into their seats. They rose when Tom's mom, who had been weepy all morning, came in, and she hugged him before she sat in her assigned place.

When everyone was assembled, Mrs. Wright was escorted to her chair, the signal for the ceremony to begin. Standing together, the cousins faced the back of the room while Dad played something slow and soft on the piano. Jenny entered the room first, in a red-sashed gold gown, and when he saw her, Chase whooped and jumped out of Aunt Muriel's arms, running to his mother.

Laughing, Jenny picked him up and gave him a kiss. Then she gave him back to Muriel and finished her walk to the front.

Dad started the Wedding March, and both mothers began to cry. Mr. Wright came in with a vision of beauty on his arm. Kata had worked magic with the simple satin gown topped by a sheer lace jacket edged with the satin material. Pam held a bouquet of red roses, and her veil was held in place with a band of silver and gold leaves. Tom couldn't take his eyes off her.

When the pair arrived at the front of the room, Mr. Wright took out his handkerchief to wipe his eyes and then shook Tom's hand and gave his daughter to him. While Jenny held Pam's flowers, the couple faced the pastor.

Somewhere in the distance, Tom heard the vows and repeated them with all his heart. He'd almost lost this beautiful being, and he knew he would have lost himself, as well, if anything had happened to her. The rings were exchanged, Jenny helped Pam lift the veil from her face, and then Tom took her in his arms while the pastor announced that they were Mr. and Mrs. Tomas Shafer and they met as one in a heartfelt kiss.

The new couple made their way with their parents to the lobby, where they formed a reception line and greeted all their guests. There were many hugs and kisses, best wishes, and congratulations to go around while the tables and chairs were rearranged in the restaurant by the staff.

Soon, they were ready to enjoy the tenderloin dinner Aunt Amelia had prepared. As champagne glasses were being filled, Hank rose from his seat. "Since I'm Best Man, I guess it's up to me to toast the happy man and wife. Tom may be my cousin, but we've been as close as brothers. Many times, growing up, getting in trouble with our other conspirator, Joe, our parents must have wondered why they had us."

"That's for sure!" Uncle Josh put in, followed by a smattering of laughter that broke out around the room.

"Pam has been like a part of the family for years. My cousin has been smitten with her since high school: she tamed him like no other, and she was his rock through the war years. In my opinion, they are as close to the perfect couple as I've ever met, and I hope, someday, to find a girl as sweet and smart as Pam. Here's to both of you and a long life together." Raising his glass to them, he was joined in the toast by everyone in the whole room.

As they were enjoying the food, Tom engaged his dad, seated across the table. "Have you set a date to leave for California, yet?"

Dad nodded. "We're going in November, mid-month."

Tom took a glance at his mother. "The liners quit coming around the first."

"We're going by air to Seattle and then catch the Daylight to Los Angeles."

"But Mom—"

His mother looked up. "Mom will bite the bullet. I don't like flying, but it's time I get over it."

Giving her a grin, he said, "Hey, maybe when you get back, I can take you up with me, finally."

The evil eye glowed. "Don't push it, mister."

Conversation buzzed around the trip until Em came over to Tom and sat in the seat Hank had just vacated. "Tom, can I ask a favor? Would it be all right if Dave and I borrowed one of the bedrooms upstairs? This would be only until we all leave for California."

Tom turned to Pam. "Would you mind?"

Laughing, she shook her head. "No. We have plenty of room up there. You're welcome to it."

Em kissed them both. "You won't even know we're there." She ran to tell Dave.

Tom put his hand on Pam's. "I'll bet it was really something when my parents had everyone up there, when they first started."

She was silent for a moment. "I'm glad we won't be alone for a while. This building can get a little spooky."

He kissed her cheek. "I'll protect you, sweetheart."

After the reception, Em and Dave settled in one of the rooms while Tom went through the theater and restaurant making sure all the outside doors were locked. When he was sure everything was secure, he headed upstairs. He had no trouble thinking "our bedroom" because they were a couple now.

Tom opened the door to a dark room and there, standing by one of the windows, bathed in the city's glow and moonlight, was his angel, the breeze lightly blowing the curtains around her. She wore a filmy white gown that hid nothing, and her golden hair cast a soft light. Tom blew a shaky breath. "My Alaskan Angel," he breathed, swelling painfully against the zipper of his trousers.

Gliding over to him almost like a phantom, her arms encircled his neck, her lips found his, and there was nothing unreal about their kiss. Pressing tight against his body, she gave a moan of pleasure in her throat, then pulled back and stroked his crotch. "That has to be uncomfortable," she teased. "Come, let me help you." And she unwrapped him as gleefully as a child tearing open a Christmas present.

"My, you're forward for a new bride," he

whispered hoarsely. When she was finished, he swung her into his arms.

"Maybe because I left my virginity behind a couple of years ago. I've been craving you ever since then." He deposited her on the bed after a lengthy kiss, and helped her shed the gauzy nightdress.

"Beautiful," he breathed as he climbed in beside her and cupped her breast. The nipple peaked with desire, and she shuddered under his touch. Ministering light kisses and stroking the contours of her body with his warm hands, he brought her to vibration as though she were a finely tuned instrument.

"Take me now, love, please," she moaned. He felt he could hold out no more, so he settled between her thighs and thrust in, with the cries of mutual pleasure resounding from their mouths. She was so warm, so tight, he wanted to remain sheathed in her forever.

Instinct took over, and he rocked back and forth in the primitive rhythm of love. Ascending to the peak, there was no one in the world except this being responding in kind to him. She shook beneath him and called out her ecstasy, triggering his orgasm, a feeling as large as the A-bomb blast, he was sure.

Tom rolled to his side and enfolded her sweat-slicked body in his arms. "I'll love you forever."

Snuggling, she kissed him again. "I love you so much. This was magic." They repeated "this" a number of times, with a small time of regrouping in between, until sleep took them. Tom glowed with happiness to wake with her in his arms.

****

Several months later, on a Monday in mid-November, Pam had never seen such utter chaos. *It's a good thing they all got reservations for a day we are closed.* Hank, Tom, Jenny, and Pam had taken such responsibility for running the theater and restaurant that their parents had left everything up to them since the first of the month.

Today Amelia had fixed a farewell breakfast for all in honor of the California-bound six, while James had even managed to take a morning away from the radio station to see them off.

Seating themselves around the table in the restaurant, the Shafers and the Nikolaevichs looked both happy and sad at the same time. Pam would miss the ones leaving, their company and their advice.

Amelia served the egg-filled breakfast casserole, ham, French bread, and cheese, before she took her place next to James. Bowls of fruit and platters of sweet rolls graced the table, also.

When all was ready, Zeke stood, gazing at those assembled. "Before we dig in, I want to thank each and every one of you for your help and support. This is going to be a big financial gain for us, and we owe it to our family and friends. Thank you, all." And then they dug into the feast.

Jenny leaned to Pam from across the table. "Have you recovered from the trial, yet? It's only been over for a few days, now."

Pam nodded. "I feel better to know that Vic won't be out for a long time. If all goes as planned, Tom and I will be gone from the area by then."

Glancing at Tom, Jenny said sadly, "I wish you didn't have to move."

Tom shook his head. "If I want to be an airline pilot, I have to go where the work is."

Pursing her lips, Addy remarked, "It looks like this may be the last time the whole family will be around the same table."

Em agreed. "Dave and I are going to stay in Los Angeles or go back to New York."

Scott spoke up. "Don and I have been accepted to the University of Washington State next fall, on our GI bill." Putting his arm around Marita with a loving glance down at her, he continued, "She's going to wait until I get back, and then we'll get married."

There were tears in Muriel's eyes as she turned to Ivan and Kata. "Then we'll all be related."

Patting her shoulder, the big Russian said, "Kata and I have felt a part of your family for a long time."

Josh asked, "What about you, Joe?"

"I want to become a park ranger at Mount McKinley. I've always loved the outdoors."

Hank snorted. "Sis, it looks like it's just you and me running the theater, while everyone else runs around to parts unknown." He dug his elbow into Jenny's side, and she gave him a sisterly shove on his shoulder.

After breakfast, everyone helped load the luggage into the vehicles and away they went to the airfield. November snowflakes danced around the skies, and a brisk Arctic breeze reddened their cheeks and noses.

Standing together near the edge of the tarmac, Pam and Tom watched as the transport plane locked the stairs in place to the cabin. Em and Dave reached them first.

Em hugged Tom. "I hope you and Pam come to Los Angeles to live. There's a big airport there."

Tom laughed. "Maybe. Meanwhile, we'll show your big-time movie at Golden North."

While Tom shook Dave's hand, Em embraced Pam. "Dear sister, write to me often." They were both crying.

"I promise."

Josh and Muriel were next. After giving Chase back to Jenny, Muriel gave Pam a kiss on her cheek. "Thank you for everything, these past few years. You're one of the reasons the business kept going. I'm so happy you're family now."

"Just doing my part."

Josh gave her a bear hug. "Keep soldier boy in line." He laughed, then looked serious. "Take care of yourself, too."

"I will."

Putting his arms around her tenderly, Zeke smiled. "Tom picked a wonderful, brave girl to be his wife, and I've gained a daughter-in-law to be proud of."

"Thank you—Dad." His eyes misted at the words.

Her heart surged when she wished Addy goodbye. This woman was as special to her as anyone she'd ever known. Addy pulled back and looked deep into her eyes. "Take good care of my son. I know he's in good hands." She kissed her. "Write to me."

They both embraced again, tears flowing down their faces. "Bowl them over in Hollywood." Pam managed to say. She opened her parka and pulled out an airsick bag and handed it to Addy.

Addy grinned. "You know me well."

Pam, Tom, and the others watched the loved ones enter the plane and stayed until it took off and they couldn't see it anymore. Holding Pam tight against the cold, Tom said gently, "Let's go home."

Kissing him, the warmth of their love spread through her. "Those are beautiful words, my love."

They headed to the car, their whole future in front of them in this new world.

Epilogue

Dear Tom and Pam,

I finally have some time to write without dashing someplace else. I'm sorry about the quick notes you've received from me since I've been here. At least things slow down some here at Christmas.

I rejoice at the news you're expecting a little one in July. I wish I could be there, but I promise to do grandma duty when I return. Hopefully, it will be some time before you find a job after we get back, so I can enjoy the little one. Grandpa Zeke practically did handsprings when he got to that part of your letter.

You should see the huge mansion the four of us moved into in the Hollywood Hills. Josh and Muriel live on one side and we are on the other. We could possibly never see each other. It has a studio area where the fellows work on the music for the production company. Those two are even writing a new musical now, in between stints on Gold Rush. They won't tell us what it's about. And, Tom, yes, I did get a small part in the production. No chiding, now.

I know it's been a while since the Carters have been to Juneau, so I'll bring you up to date. My Aunt Jen lives in a small apartment since Uncle Henry passed on, two years ago. As far as the rest of Muriel's brothers and her sister, Casey moved his family to Reno, Nevada. He said it will be the next big boom town. Buster passed on from a cancer ten years ago. Never got married. Maggie's family lives in the San Gabriel Valley. She worked in an airplane factory out there during the war. Maybe you flew one of her planes. She's married, with four children. It's hard to think that little Maggie is a mother now. We went to Forest Lawn Cemetery to pay our respects to Grandpa and Grandma Applegate. They are in a beautiful section with a lovely fountain. I'm sure they'd be pleased.

Los Angeles has changed so much in the twenty-some years since we left. Where there were farms and orange trees is now a sprawl of city. It seems to go on forever. They're building something called a freeway that will move cars without intersections. Fancy that! Trolleys are gone, but they still have streetcars. There's little I recognize anymore.

The studio is up in the hills, too. Dan and Roxie Hanson live very close to where we are. It was so wonderful to see Roxie again. She and Ann were my dear friends at Majestic. She has two sons, and both were in the war. One lost an arm in Europe but is doing well with an artificial one. The other was a pilot like you, Tom, only he flew out of England. They both have families, so we grandparents enjoy trading stories.

As for the Giovannis, I don't think they are even here anymore. I did get a little nervous when a big black car slowed down where Muriel and I were waiting for the streetcar, and more when it came around the block again. Nothing happened, though. I'm still a bit uneasy around here, I guess. Well, I'm looking at the clock and know I still have a lot to do. We're going out to dinner tonight.

Anyway, give my love to the rest of the family. The presents for Christmas should be on their way. I miss all of you so. Have a very Merry Christmas and a bright New Year!

Love to all,
Mom and Dad

Thank you for purchasing
this Wild Rose Press publication.
For other wonderful stories of romance,
please visit our on-line bookstore at
www.thewildrosepress.com

For questions or more information,
contact us at
info@thewildrosepress.com

The Wild Rose Press
www.TheWildRosePress.com

To visit with authors of The Wild Rose Press
join our yahoo loop at
http://groups.yahoo.com/group/thewildrosepress/